A Taste of Her

A short story collection

by

Tiana Warner

Rogue Cannon Publishing
BC, Canada

ISBN: 978-1-7782651-0-5

tianawarner.com

Also by Tiana Warner:

The Valkyrie's Daughter
*A sapphic YA Fantasy with a slow-burn
enemies-to-lovers romance.*

From Fan to Forever
An age-gap lesbian celebrity romance.

Cougar Woods (Eternally Hers collection)
An age-gap lesbian paranormal shifter romance novella.

Mermaids of Eriana Kwai Series
Ice Massacre
Ice Crypt
Ice Kingdom
*A YA Fantasy trilogy with a friends-to-enemies-to-lovers
romance between a warrior girl and a mermaid.*

See all of Tiana Warner's books at tianawarner.com

These Glittering Treasures

*A pirate captain returns to plunder her favorite port, where she and
a ravishing young lady play a familiar game.*

While my crew works to moor *The Santiago*, an impressive
galleon we "borrowed" from the Armada three months
ago, I hop onto the creaking dock with a pistol in hand.

Swaying with the waves, I inhale deeply, a grin on my
lips. The tropical air is thick and warm, teasing me with
the smell of spices, sugar, and other luxuries.

It's good to be back. Of all the towns in the Spanish
Main, there's something seductive about this one's
treasures, charm, buildings… and yes, the people.

While my first mate, Diego, pays off the harbor-master with silver, I stride past a few fishing vessels and pause to steady my feet on the firm ground.

"Take what you can until I give the word, boys!" I shout, waving my pistol. "Gold, liquor, food—and don't forget soap this time, for God's sake."

My crew rushes onto the land with cheers and roars, ready to pilfer as much as this town has to offer. "Aye, Captain!"

As they rush into the streets, civilians notice their guests and run for cover in the brick and wood buildings. Screams, barking dogs, and braying mules rise in a chorus.

I'm keen to be rid of the boys for a while. I love them like brothers, and like any good siblings, they annoy the hell out of me. In the long days at sea, I often wish for the company of other women—but unfortunately, few who are sane choose a life of piracy.

While panic erupts, I dash through the streets to my familiar target: the extravagant brick towers that make up the House of Méndez. My heart pounds with the anticipation of what's inside.

I shoot the lock on the door with a clang of metal on metal, then kick the door open with a flourish. "Lovely day for a pillage!" I sing. "Miss me?"

The House's three servants clamber back, their expressions taut with surprise. One of them drops a pile of washing.

Before they get any ideas about a show of courage, I walk inside and fire a shot into the ceiling. "Everybody out! Come on."

Wood fragments shower down, and the servants flee into the street, screaming.

Beneath the residual gun powder, the home smells mouth-watering, like freshly baked cake. I'll have to remember to grab something to eat on the way out.

Nobody else comes to meet me.

My lips curl into a grin. If the man of the house isn't here, that gives me time.

I race up the stairs, checking in every room, before arriving at a closed door.

I draw a breath, ready my pistol, and enter.

The bedroom is the same as I remember it, from the gold cushions on the bed to the ornate dressing screen. A young lady stands beside the writing desk at the back of the room, her delicate hand gripping the back of a wooden chair.

My stomach swoops, a sensation like cresting a wave at sea.

She's in a black dress with gold embroidery, which flatters her tan skin and dark hair... but I will never understand fashion. Yes, the bodice gives her waist a tantalizing shape, and the ornamentation is lovely, but the dress has so many layers of skirts that it hides her shape from the waist down.

Women's legs should not be hidden. If I were responsible for fashion, we would all be in trousers.

"Señorita Antonia!" I lower my pistol and shut the door behind me. "What a lovely surprise."

Antonia laughs, a glint in her emerald eyes. "Captain Lucia. How convenient that you've arrived when my parents are out."

I step closer. "Lucky timing."

She lifts an eyebrow, stepping back until she's leaning against the desk. "Or planned."

I grin, then remember my courtesies and bow. "You look ravishing today."

"And you look... like you've been at sea for a while."

I lift my chin and run a hand down my sand-colored braid. "That may be true, but I'll have you know that I bathed this morning for the occasion and am wearing my finest attire."

"So it would seem. Isn't that my dear cousin Carlos's jacket?"

I look down at it, feigning surprise. "Well, I suppose it is."

Antonia sighs, peeking between her fluttering curtains to the chaos in the streets. "There's no point in protesting, is there?"

I stride closer. I would tell her that I regret having to steal from her, but that would be a lie. "No. What've you got for me today?"

She doesn't move, so I keep advancing until we're nose-to-nose. Her breath hitches, and her gaze flicks down my body and back to my face.

She smells as sweet as the town she lives in, like cocoa and cinnamon. Her soft, smooth skin is easier on the eyes than any of the haggard men I'm forced to look at every day.

"Did your father bring you gifts since we last met?" I ask quietly.

"Chocolates," she whispers. "A crystal pendant. Silk stockings."

"Silk… stockings?" I say, mouth dry.

"Yes." Her rosy lips curve upward. "You might not be familiar, given your choice of trousers and other men's fashion, but—"

"I know what stockings are," I snap.

"Do you want to see?" She wiggles her shoulders in a way that makes heat rush to my cheeks.

She grows bolder every time I see her.

"I—well—are you wearing them?" I ask. Any control I had over this situation is slipping through my fingers.

She nods.

More heat. I back up a step. "I'll take the pendant and chocolates."

"Very well." She brushes past, and a ripple travels up my arm as we touch.

As she rummages through her wardrobe, I steady myself with a deep breath. Beyond the closed door, the house is dead quiet, and Antonia's every movement is sharp in my ears. For now, it's just us. Everything going on in the streets is a world away.

She returns with the treasures I asked for, and our fingers graze as she passes them to me.

Smiling, I bow. "With respect, you are probably the easiest person to steal from, señorita."

Antonia chews her bottom lip. "You're right. My father will be disappointed that I handed over his gifts so readily."

She backs up toward the writing desk, something teasing in her expression. It sends a flutter through me, and I step closer without meaning to.

She puts her wrists together and offers them to me. "Aren't you going to restrain me, Captain?"

I swallow hard. Seven times, we've met, and seven times, she's played this game with me—wanting to be endangered so she can be rescued. I can't help but go along with it. She's too beautiful to refuse, even if toying with her is a waste of time.

"If you insist, love." I put my loot on the bed, then push her into the wooden chair and grab a pale pink ribbon from the desk. It's cool and smooth between my fingers. "Silk?"

"Yes."

"Valuable. I might have to take this, as well."

The silk stockings beneath her dress take form in my imagination, and I scowl, turning my attention to my hands.

Antonia grins, watching my face as I loop the ribbon over her wrists. My fingers graze her soft forearms.

Standing over her, I avoid meeting her eye, but my gaze draws to the swell of her breasts under her bodice.

She hisses as I cinch the ribbon tight and knot it. I let her bound hands fall into her lap.

"There you are. Restrained by a pirate, and you could do nothing to stop her from taking your prized possessions." I lean down, putting my hands on the arm rests. "One day, love, you'll get tired of playing the damsel. What's going to happen when this town runs out of handsome men to rescue you? Or is there one who keeps returning?"

She tilts her head and opens her mouth, but no sound comes out. Is she suddenly shy?

How unlike her.

She bites her lip. I catch myself doing the same. Does she know what she does to me?

There's a crash behind us as the bedroom door flies open.

Antonia gasps.

I spin around, my pistol raised.

Diego is there, a wicked grin on his lips.

"We takin' hostages this time? Good." He strides over and grabs Antonia's bound wrists, pulling her to her feet. "What else you got? Is that crystal?"

"Let go of me!" Antonia shouts, all playfulness gone from her tone.

"We are *not* taking hostages," I say, jabbing Diego in the chest with my pistol. A sick feeling twists inside me.

If he knew what I was thinking… if he knew the hold this lady has over me…

"Come off it," he growls, pushing away the barrel without flinching. "We've got enough trinkets to fill eight ships. We need leverage if we want *gold*, Captain."

He raises Antonia's wrists and shakes them like she's a sack of coins he found.

Antonia's eyes are wide with fear. She works her wrists, trying to come free of the ribbon, and I regret tying it so tight.

"Diego, let go of her. No hostages."

He rolls his eyes and steps toward the door, pulling Antonia so she stumbles after him.

I point my pistol at him. "I'm going to count to three, and if you survive the gunshot to your head, I'll drag you back to the ship and keelhaul you until the last thing you see is your own blood clouding the harbor."

I'd do it, too. Yes, they are my brothers, but a firm hand is the only way a captain stays a captain.

Diego faces me, and whatever he sees in my eyes makes that wicked grin slide off his face.

He lets go of Antonia and puts his hands up. "All right, all right. You're the boss."

"And you shouldn't need reminding of it, you filthy bilge rat. Get outside and find some of those *trinkets* you think you're too good for. I'll be out soon."

Diego stomps away, and I slam the door behind him and lock it. The moment his footsteps retreat down the stairs, I holster my weapon and rush to Antonia's side.

"I'm so sorry," I say, fumbling with the ribbon. "Are you okay, love?"

She stares at me, calm and steady. "Captain Lucia, I never understand you. You're a *pirate*. You're supposed to pillage, not rescue the damsel."

I meet her emerald eyes and silently curse my heart for skipping a beat.

I cast her a teasing grin. "So, you admit it. You love being a damsel."

"I—well, yes. When I act a certain way, men dote on me and buy me everything I ask for. It's wonderful."

"And in return, you let them bed you?"

"Excuse you!" she cries, affronted. "I am an unmarried woman of nineteen and have never been with a man in *that way*."

I bite my lip. For reasons I don't care to admit, the idea of her never having been with a man excites me.

"Anyway, don't change the topic," she says. "Why did you rescue me? Why are you so good to me whenever you come here?"

She must know why. But I refuse to say it.

Avoiding her eye, I finish untying her and let the pink ribbon flutter to the floor.

She stares at me, waiting.

I open my mouth, searching for words. "There's no sense in taking you hostage. You have a lot of pretty things I need to steal before I *actually* endanger your life, señorita."

I turn away. Of course I wouldn't let anyone take her from her home. She's safe and comfortable here, and it needs to stay that way. She's too sweet and gentle for the sea.

"What's that necklace you're wearing?" she asks.

"What?"

Her boots tap closer. "Turn around. Show me."

Damn her. She's tipped me off-balance and knows it.

My face is surely the color of a lobster, but I turn. When I don't produce the necklace from beneath my tunic, she reaches forward and grabs it herself.

"My emerald pendant," she says. "I knew it. You kept it."

I tug it back and put it beneath my tunic. "It's lovely. I didn't want to sell it."

"Uh-huh. And what other items of mine have you kept instead of selling?"

I make a choking sound, unable to articulate anything.

"Don't be embarrassed," Antonia says. "I think it's sweet that you kept them."

"Sweet? I've done nothing but steal from you! You should be repulsed by me!"

"And yet, you just rescued me."

"Because I—"

"What?" She steps closer, her face so close to mine that her breath tickles my lips. "Admit it."

My insides flip, as unsteady as if I'm sailing through a storm.

I scowl, keeping my lips shut tight. I refuse to be ridiculed for falling in love with a beautiful lady like Antonia. She's an upper-class woman with a promising future as the wife of a wealthy man. I'm the lowest class of society and doomed to stay that way.

I'm wrong to keep coming here and playing like this. If I care about her, I'll let her live a normal life and stop pillaging her home like a scoundrel.

I take the chocolates and crystal pendant, and back up toward the door, knowing what I have to do. "My crew is waiting."

Antonia softens, her shoulders dropping. "Captain Lucia, wait."

"No. You've delayed me for long enough."

"But—"

I raise a hand, continuing toward the door. "You're right. I'm a pirate, and I've forgotten my place in the world. This is the last time you'll see me."

"Lucia, you stop right now," Antonia says firmly.

I stop. It's the first time she's addressed me without my title.

She gathers her skirts, marches forward, and catches my chin in her soft fingers. She guides my face toward hers, and kisses me hard on the lips.

My body reacts without my permission, grabbing her waist and kissing her back.

Then my brain catches up, and I push her away. "What are you doing?"

"The thing you've been too shy to do for two years! You keep coming back here, even though I'm certain you can get much better treasures elsewhere, and I have gotten to know you as well as a suitor over this time. I am delighted to see you every time you break my door down, and I *want* you to see my silk stockings, and I don't know why we don't just admit that we love each other!"

There's a ringing silence. We stand a stride apart, unmoving. Antonia catches her breath like she's just run a long distance.

Her last words loop in my mind. *We love each other.*

"You do?" I ask, relaxing my grip on my loot.

"Yes!" She bends her knees, like this topic is pushing her to her limits. "You are the most exciting thing to happen in my life, and you make me feel like I have worth, in some strange way. The way you look at me and really *see* me is like…" She huffs, color rising in her cheeks.

It's like I've been standing on a cliff, postponing the moment I have to jump into the water, but now the last rock has crumbled beneath my boots, and I have no choice but to leap.

I grab her and kiss her, pulling her against me. The chocolates and pendant crash to the floor.

Antonia kisses me back hungrily, her hands moving beneath my jacket and around to the small of my back.

I break our kiss to meet her gaze. "Never speak of this," I whisper.

"If you insist," she murmurs.

I walk her back toward the bed, where I push her down and climb on top of her.

She's an irresistible sight, with her dark hair spread across the pillows, flushed cheeks, and parted lips. Her breast rises and falls, and her eyes… God, those beautiful green eyes.

Her hands link around my neck and I lean down to kiss her. I can hardly bear the feel of her body beneath mine, with her soft curves and her legs parted beneath her skirts.

I reach down and pull her skirts up, tentatively.

"Lucia," she whispers, breathing faster. She reaches beneath my tunic and caresses my waist, so gentle.

I lift her skirts enough to expose her undergarments— those achingly beautiful silk stockings. They're the color of pearls. I run my hands over them, memorizing the feel of her legs beneath my palms, before sliding down the stockings and tossing them aside.

Her legs are perfect—even more than I imagined.

"Lucia, I've wanted this for so long," she says, tugging my tunic.

I shed my jacket and remove my tunic, a flutter in my chest. "Me, as well."

I lay on top of her, kissing her tenderly while sliding a hand between her legs. The sound she makes is so sweet that I close my eyes to savor it.

Her hands trace over my breasts, and she pinches my nipples.

I gasp. "Oh, that feels good."

She grins. We kiss deeper, moving against each other. The feel of her against my breasts is tantalizing.

"Can I try something?" I whisper.

Antonia nods, a spark in her eyes.

I crawl lower on the bed and lift her skirts over my head, settling into the darkness between her legs.

"Captain Lucia," she says playfully, "what are you—"

She gasps as I run my hands up her thighs to the apex between her legs. There, I kiss her gently.

She cries out, and satisfaction surges through me. I close my eyes and kiss her again. I lick her up and down, side to side, until she trembles and goosebumps ripple up her legs.

"Lucia... I didn't know anything could feel so amazing," she says, gasping.

I lick her faster, lost in the taste of her and the feel of her legs around me. Heat coils inside me.

I push her thighs apart, moving my tongue faster. Her moans grow louder, and soon—

"Oh... oh... Lucia... I..."

She shivers, and calls out loudly enough that I'm sure people must hear us in the streets.

I surface from her skirts and lay beside her, grinning. Her hair is a mess, like she's been pulling it, and her cheeks are flushed.

"Where did you learn that?" she asks, panting.

"I've sailed to every corner of the earth, love. The things I've heard about on my travels would make you blush. But I admit… I've imagined trying a few of those things on you."

She props up on her elbows. "Oh? What else have you wanted to try?"

I grin and roll onto my back, pulling her on top of me. "If you're fine with my crew ransacking the town for another hour or two, I can show you."

The Tasting Room

When a woman applies for a job at a winery, the tension between her and the owner turns the interview into something more.

I've decided how today will end: either I get the job and move five hours away from home, or I don't get the job and find another way to move five hours away from home.

God, I hope it's the first one.

I park my Prius in the winery's gravel lot, my heart thumping so hard it's like it's trying to escape my chest.

My parents are upset but they can't be surprised. I'm twenty-three, and it's time to move out. A new life and some distance will give me a chance to figure out some things—like how to get over the woman I thought I would propose to.

Beyond my windshield, the main building could be a refurbished old barn or a brand new structure designed to look rustic. It's charming and reminds me of visiting my grandpa's ranch growing up. Wine barrels flank the entrance, and the wooden sign overhead says *Dubois Estate* in cursive. Behind it, the vineyard dips and curves with the landscape, a blip of paradise on the dry Washington hillside.

As I get out of the car, the searing August heat beats down on me, and I rush to the entrance. I've already got a nervous sweat threatening to show on my white blouse; I don't need the sun to speed up the process.

When I walk in, the aromas of wood and wine mingle in my nose. The room is spacious under a vaulted ceiling, with wine and merchandise arranged neatly along the walls. The air conditioning makes my skin tingle.

A middle-aged man greets me from behind the bar on the other side of the vast room.

"I'm here for an interview?" I say, the words coming out like a question. Like I'm half expecting him to respond "no."

"You must be Kiera. Just a minute."

He leaves me standing in the hollow silence, listening to my shallow breaths. I smooth my hair, frame the dark locks around my face, and adjust the white blouse and gray suit that I bought for the occasion.

Why do interviews have to be so stressful? Is it because we've connected them to survival? *Get the job, earn money, acquire food and shelter. Fail the interview, be unemployed, starve and die.*

Great, this is helping.

"Stop it," I whisper. "There are plenty of job opportunities."

And that's the moment the man returns with someone.

Please tell me they didn't hear me talking to myself.

My gaze locks onto my interviewer, and my heart skips a beat. I've met her before.

What was her name?

She's a few years older than me, tall, slim, an image of elegance. Her sleek brunette hair is combed back, leaving me to linger on her hazel eyes and the sharp angles of her face. Her black suit, red heels, and ruby lipstick pop against her pale skin.

"Marie Dubois," she says with a hint of a French accent in the way she purrs her name.

We shake hands.

Marie.

Her voice sparks something inside me. When we met at the music festival five years ago, that low purr tipped my attraction over the edge, making me take her hand and dance my heart out to an indie band that was mediocre at best. Her captivating eyes, her confidence, and her carefree laugh made me dream of her for months afterwards. She'd been bold, forward, seductive. I was figuring out my sexuality at the time, and oh, did she ever help me learn what I wanted.

Wait, did she say her last name is Dubois? *The* Dubois?

"Y-you're the owner?" I stammer.

This is doing nothing for my nerves. I expected to interview with an employee, not the winery owner.

Her gaze traces over me in a way that makes my stomach flutter. Her ruby lips curve in the slightest smile, and she motions for me to follow her into the back room.

I don't think she remembers me. Maybe that's for the best. The fact that we grinded on each other in bikinis five years ago isn't exactly professional.

She leads me to an office and shuts the door. The furniture is simple, the desk and chairs made of reclaimed wood, an abstract painting that might be a mountain range on the opposite wall.

I sit in a chair, and she perches on the desk in front of me. I don't know if it's a power move or if she's trying to seem casual, but the closeness makes my pulse accelerate. She's towering over me, our knees almost touching, and I can smell her sweet perfume.

"My grandparents started this business before I was born," she purrs. "I inherited it and have taken it to the status we're at today. More awards, more revenue, more influential visitors than ever. My staff has to be dedicated to my vision. Are you up to the challenge?"

"Yes ma'am." God, this woman has the confidence of someone who's been doing this for decades, but she's only in her twenties.

She smiles, and the look is so beautiful on her that it takes the breath from my lungs. "Don't call me ma'am." Her gaze sweeps over me again. "You're very pretty, Kiera. I think you'd be a nice face behind the bar. Why do you want this job?"

"I have a passion for wine," I say, my answer coming automatically after so much time rehearsing this question. "My customer service background—"

"No. Why do you really want it? Your resume says you're from Seattle. Why would a city girl want to move all the way out here?"

I open and close my mouth, caught off-guard. How am I supposed to answer this without spilling my personal life about getting cheated on? Do I tell her I want to get away from everyone I've ever known and start a new life?

No. That is *not* a job interview conversation.

"I've… found myself in a position where I can build my life anywhere I want. I want to move away from the city and start an interesting career. Something that speaks to me. Something I'd be good at."

She bites her lip while her gaze traces over me. "I don't know why anyone would want to move away from the city."

This seems like a strange thing to say. "Why not?"

"This vineyard is beautiful, yes. I have dogs and horses, yes. But where do I go to make friends, try fancy restaurants, meet a new lover?"

Heat rises in my face. I shift on the hard wooden seat. "There must be bars and clubs—"

"There's one bar," she says, raising a manicured finger. Her hands are smooth and delicate. "Tell me, do you want to move to a town where there's one bar and it's full of old men who want to cheat on their wives with you?"

Maybe it's the mention of cheating, but her words ignite something spiteful in my chest. "I don't want to be with any men, never mind cheating ones," I say sharply.

She leans back, raising her eyebrows a fraction. "We met before. Remind me where."

My mouth goes dry. So she does recognize me. "Music festival. Seattle. Five years ago."

Her eyes light up, and for a moment, she's the girl who was wearing heart-shaped sunglasses and a pink bikini. We danced in the sun, our sweaty bodies grinding, our noses brushing, the air between us thick with something new and exciting. If I let my mind wander there, I can still smell her coconut sunscreen. We never kissed, but God, I wanted to feel her lips on mine.

The memory strikes me in a flash, and then her playful expression is gone, and her face returns to the cool confidence of a winery owner.

"So why would you want to move here, Kiera? Why would you move away from the coast, where you have music festivals and the beach?"

"Why don't you move to the city, if you don't like it here?" I challenge, cocking an eyebrow.

She grips the edge of the desk with her delicate fingers, rocking a little, like she's contemplating my words. "I like it here. The job. The space. I just wish for more. I don't want you to take this job if you're not aware of what you will be giving up. I've lost people to this very thing. There's no Space Needle in this part of Washington."

"But there's nature. Peace and quiet. Different opportunities that I can't get in the city."

She studies me, her gaze sending a tendril of heat through my midsection. Whatever she's thinking makes a flush creep into her cheeks, and she clears her throat.

"And what attracts you to my winery, of all places?" she asks, not meeting my eye.

"Your reputation. I used to work at a steakhouse, and your wine was the best on the menu."

She sits taller, and I silently congratulate myself for flattering her.

She could be a painting, the way she's perched on the desk, all curves and poise. She knows she runs a good business, and it's evident in the way she holds her head and unapologetically takes up space.

I'm staring. I drop my gaze to the wooden desk, where her fingers tap a rhythm on the edge.

Silence stretches between us.

"You disappeared that day," I say quietly. "I never learned anything about you except your first name."

She studies me before answering. "I was only visiting Seattle for the festival. I hitchhiked to get there. My parents didn't know until it was too late."

A breath of laughter escapes. "You must have been in big trouble."

"I was grounded for a month when I got home." She sighs, holding my gaze. "It was worth it. Just to get away from here and see the city for a weekend."

Interesting. I imagine her growing up on this vineyard, stuck here, dreaming of city life.

"Did your parents keep close tabs on you?" I ask.

"I wasn't allowed to go anywhere, never mind the big city."

This explains her doubts about why anyone would leave urban life to come work here. She's spent her life stuck on this plot of land. This career was probably part of her future from the day she was born.

But I've spent my life stuck in the city. This vineyard calls my name, and so does a peaceful life far from everything I've ever known. I need something new.

"If…" I clear my throat. "If you had lived in the city, would you have asked for my number that day?"

My lips tingle as the words come out. Maybe it's inappropriate to ask. But I need to know. I've needed to know for years.

A flush rises in her cheeks.

"Yes. I think I would have." She drops her gaze, her brow furrowed. "Do you ever wonder what would've happened between us if I didn't need to leave that day?"

"All the time," I say without hesitating.

She stops tapping her fingers on the desk. The room is silent. She leans closer, her face hovering inches from mine.

"My employees are involved in the winemaking process." Her timbre lowers to a purr that makes me shiver. "Are you good with your hands?"

"Very good," I say, my mouth dry.

The way she's sitting on the edge of the desk, leaning close, I have to tilt my head to meet her gaze. The ghost of a smile pulls at her ruby lips, and it's the same playful one I fell hard for five years ago.

"And you have a palate for wine?" she asks.

"I'm also good with my tongue if that's what you're asking."

Oh my *God*, did I really just say that?

What am I doing, saying these things to my potential employer? This is not the same girl I wanted to kiss while we were in bikinis five years ago. This is an *interview*.

She stares at me, her expression unreadable.

This is a disaster. Time to thank her and get out of here. Maybe there's another winery in the area that's open to interviewing me today.

I clear my throat. "I'm sorry. That was—"

"Do you want to show me what you mean?" she murmurs.

Oh.

The room suddenly feels a lot smaller. Her knee grazes mine. Have we been sitting this close the whole time or did we both lean in?

Her perfume is intoxicating. I drop my gaze to her lips, something primal threatening to overtake me.

Beyond the door, a bell chimes, and conversation erupts. We both start, like we've forgotten where we were.

Marie's gaze darts to the clock on the wall. It's rustic and trendy like everything else about this building. "I have a party to entertain."

My insides hollow out. "Right. Of course."

But she definitely made an advance a second ago, right? Is she regretting her words? Maybe she suddenly remembered that this is an interview, and flirting is a terrible idea.

Heat builds in my face. Ugh, was that really an interview? I didn't even get to tell her about my strengths and weaknesses, or a time I solved a problem at work.

I get up and step toward the door, flustered.

"Let me," Marie says, hurrying ahead. She stops with a hand on the door. "Kiera, I like your resume. It's why I called you here. I'm sorry if I…"

We're standing close together, the air crackling between us.

"I hope you're not sorry," I say, the words barely a whisper. I'm not sorry at all. I'm embarrassed and confused, sure, but I don't regret letting her know that I never got over her.

Her ruby lips part, and her sweet breath tickles my face. Her chest rises and falls more rapidly. There's a flash of uncertainty behind her eyes, the first glimpse of something other than total confidence. She cups a cool hand to my cheek, leans in…

And our lips meet in a gentle, teasing kiss. It's the kiss I've dreamed about since we met, and it's better than I imagined. Her lips are full, her taste is sweet, and it sends a tingle all the way through me.

I feel her pulling back, as if she's ready to gauge my reaction or apologize, but I don't want the kiss to be over. I slide my hands around her waist, pull her close, and kiss her deeper.

She lets out a breath, softening in my arms. Her fingers move through my hair, sending a rush of pleasure down my back.

Our lips move faster. My breath hitches. I slide my hands beneath her suit jacket, holding her against me.

She walks me back a step, pinning me against the door. The sensation of her body against mine makes me dizzy—her full lips, her playful tongue, her breasts, stomach, and hips. Heat builds inside me as her fingers explore my body.

Since the music festival, whenever I thought of Marie, I tried to convince myself that I liked the idea of her more than anything. I told myself she was a fantasy I built up in my head, making her out to be more than she really was. After all, I never even knew her last name.

But kissing her now, I know my idea of her wasn't a fantasy. She's real, and here, and the taste and feel of her are absolute bliss.

We move against each other, our breaths coming fast, soft moans escaping. Her fingers dig into me, and I grip her shirt, aching to feel her skin against mine.

She trails her soft fingers down my chest and pops open a button of my blouse, making me gasp. She circles a hand over my breast, teasing me with the layers of fabric between us.

Dizzy with need, I tug her shirt up and run my hand over the bare skin at her waist. She lets out a moan.

Beyond the door, the group of guests erupts in laughter, and someone's footsteps click closer.

Marie and I stop kissing, panting.

The footsteps stop, and we hold our breaths. Her fingers tighten in my hair.

"Marie will be just a moment," the man who greeted me calls out. He's inches away, just beyond the closed door. "She's in a meeting. Can I get you anything in the meantime?"

His footsteps retreat.

With regret in her eyes, Marie steps back.

I let out a breath and wipe my lips, which I'm sure are covered in ruby lipstick.

"I'm sorry. I do have to go," she says, smoothing her brunette hair with delicate fingers.

I can't speak. My insides are erupting with the heat of that kiss. I want more.

Buttoning my shirt with trembling fingers, I manage to say, "Sounds like a lot of customers out there. You might not live near a city, Marie, but you still get to meet a lot of people. I'd like to try this life. I think it would suit me."

Marie says nothing. When I meet her hazel eyes, she's smiling.

My heart skips.

"Good," she says. "I think you'll fit in well at this job, Kiera."

City Girl

A new girl in town meets someone cute at the dog park, but her rambunctious pup makes the situation more awkward by the minute.

The dog park is supposed to be a good place to meet people. Everyone told me the same—my parents, sister, bestie, and anyone else who's heard me gripe about how hard it is to make friends in Los Angeles.

"Be bold and get out there!" they all said.

Well, my disaster of a dog is rolling around on a dead fish, and I don't know who's going to talk to me when my supposed conversation starter is covered in decayed salmon.

"Moose, no! Come here." I race down the beach, heat rising in my face.

He's led three other dogs to the jackpot and they're all rubbing their chests in it. Their owners race over, shouting and cursing. We become a tangle of limbs as we try to catch our pets.

"Sorry," I stammer. "I'm so sorry. He's a hound mix… when he catches a scent he's relentless…"

"No worries," a guy grumbles, his tone saying otherwise as Moose knocks him sideways.

Ugh, I should give up hope of making friends or finding a girlfriend in the city. I can't believe I put on makeup for this.

I lunge for Moose, who thinks I'm playing and jumps up. He plants two muddy paws on my chest.

"Get off! You smell like hot garbage."

He barks and zooms in a wide circle, apparently thrilled by all of this chaos. Other dogs follow him until the park is a furry vortex.

Okay, my dog is officially a terror, and I can never show my face here again.

With a huff, I shrug out of my backpack, then take off my flannel shirt and tie it around my waist. The clear spring morning is chilly, but a t-shirt is better than standing here with muddy paw prints on my boobs. I gather my blond locks into a messy ponytail, giving up on looking nice.

When I shoulder my backpack again, it smudges mud on my t-shirt. I sigh and look skyward.

Someone shouts behind me. An English bulldog with an underbite trundles toward the fish, and across the muddy field near the park entrance, his owner sprints toward us, arms waving.

They'll never make it in time to stop the bulldog.

Not wanting anyone else to suffer as I have, I grab the chonky pup before he lands on the fish, scooping him up like a football. I hold him, trying to keep other dogs back with my knees, while his owner catches up, panting.

"Good snag. I thought I'd have to go to work smelling like a dead fish."

As I hand over the squirming bulldog, I lift my gaze to a pair of light brown eyes. My heart stumbles.

"My—my pleasure," I say, my lips tingling. "I already smell like a dead fish, so…"

Smooth, Meg.

The bulldog's owner takes him from me and sets him down away from the offending fish. "I'm Ava. They/she."

"Meg," I say. "She/her."

Wow, an introduction! That's the closest I've come to making a friend at a dog park. Okay, time to retreat in shame and never come back.

Except…

A couple of inches taller than me, Ava traces their gaze over me in a way that makes my belly flutter. They're rocking a black button-down shirt with the sleeves rolled up, relaxed-fit jeans, and a bold leather watch. Their dark hair is buzzed on the sides and wavy on top, perfectly styled. The contrast of their feminine makeup and masculine clothing makes my knees weak. Is it suddenly hot out?

"I—I was just going to head home and give my dog a bath," I say.

Moose barks, demanding my attention. I peel my gaze from Ava to find him chest-deep in the waves, wanting to play fetch.

"I think your dog has other plans," Ava says with a cute twist of their lips. Their voice tingles pleasantly in my ears, smooth and calming.

Flushed, I find the nearest stick and chuck it into the water. Moose and several other dogs chase it, and Ava's bulldog lumbers after them.

"I guess the salt water will help clean him off," I say begrudgingly.

"It's happened before at this park," Ava says, glancing at the dead salmon. "A bit unavoidable on the beach."

I grimace at the yapping vortex. "All dog parks are so out of control. I kind of hate them because you never know who or what you'll find."

Moose returns and drops the stick on my shoes. I throw it again.

"You hate dog parks?" Ava asks.

"I mean—no—I love dogs. And parks. But I'd rather go somewhere more controlled and... predictable..." I shut my mouth before I say something else that comes out wrong.

Ava shrugs. "I like the chaos. It's exciting."

A breeze wafts the fish smell in our direction, triggering my gag reflex. "Should we, um, move away from…?"

"Yeah."

We shuffle sideways a few paces.

"I would just rather not get muddy and frazzled before work," I say, trying to redeem myself so I don't come off as a fun-hater.

"Is that why you moved to the city? Work?" Ava asks.

"How'd you know I moved to the city?"

"I come to this park every morning and have never seen you here. Also, the patch on your backpack tells me you went to high school in the burbs."

I automatically glance at the patch. *The Wildcats*. My high school volleyball team. "Perceptive."

"I'm a detective."

"Really?"

"No."

I laugh. *Cute.*

The bulldog returns to Ava and sits, leaning against their calf.

Ava rubs his ear. "Good boy, Pretzel. Go play a bit."

"Pretzel," I echo, putting a hand over my heart.

Ava flashes a stunning smile. "My six-year-old nephew came up with it."

Moose races up, and after a year with him, I know him well enough to read his body language: he is about to greet Ava with all four paws and a tongue.

"Don't!" I shout, diving between them.

Pretzel yips and scoots away.

I grab Moose around the middle and knock him aside, which he takes as permission to roughhouse. He comes back at me with a vengeance, his front paws batting, his haunches tucking under him for a burst of speed.

Ugh, the indignity of fending off my own dog like this.

There's mud on my boobs again, and I've run out of layers to shed. I'm never returning here.

"Go bug the other dogs!" I say, stumbling as I try to stop him from ruining Ava's clothes.

"Another good save—oops!" Ava catches me around the waist and holds me upright, saving me from toppling into mud that's had God-knows-what in it.

"Thanks," I say, panting.

Their breath tickles my lips. My pulse races at the closeness. Their arms are warm and strong around me, and I have the ridiculous urge to just stay like this. They smell like lavender, which is blissful after suffering through a whiff of Moose a moment ago.

A husky bounds over, and Moose diverts his attention to his new friend. How come he's having such an easy time making friends and I'm over here drowning in awkwardness?

Ava lets go of me and steps back. If I'm not mistaken, they look a little flustered. Was it the unintentional embrace or are they upset that I got mud on them?

"What job brought you here?" they ask.

"I'm a rocket scientist."

"Really?"

"No."

Ava grins, their smile contagious. "Walked into that, didn't I?"

"Yup." I try not to stare, but God, Ava's cute. Could all of the idiots who told me to try and meet people at a dog park actually be right? "I'm a software developer. Satellite company."

Ava faces me fully. "Seriously? That's cool."

People always say that, but the work is hardly thrilling, and I don't click with any of my coworkers. "Mm, I don't know. I write code, they pay me, I go home. It's…"

"Controlled and predictable?"

I purse my lips. "Got me."

We step back as a horde of dogs barrels through, Moose and the husky in the lead, Pretzel yapping at their haunches.

"So you think I should embrace more chaos in my life?" I ask. Maybe my routine is my problem. Maybe friends and relationships come to you when you do bold and outgoing things—like when I met that super hot Australian girl while on a ski trip a couple of years ago. I was a different person on that trip, social, flirty, unrestrained. That bold side of me got a girl, at least for the night.

Ava laughs. "I think you should do whatever makes you happy, Meg."

I smile, liking the sound of my name on their lips.

"Up until a couple of years ago, I wanted to be an astronaut," Ava says.

It's a miracle they're still talking to me. Hasn't my rambunctious dog and the lingering smell scared them off?

"What stopped you from going after that dream?" I ask.

Ava searches my face, making me wonder what they're thinking. Seeming to realize they're staring, they shift their attention to the canine juggernaut racing around the park. I do too, wishing my face would stop burning up.

A few strides away, the guy who grumbled at me is using a branch to push the dead salmon into the ocean. I pretend to be interested in what he's doing.

"I was... afraid," Ava says. "It's a lot of work, and even if I give it my all, there's still a good chance I'd fail."

"I get that," I say. "Rejection sucks. I got rejected by eighteen companies before landing this job."

"*Eighteen?*"

"Most of the positions I applied for were out of my league."

"That's... brave."

I return their little smile. "Even if you don't go into space, you could apply for a related job. It's worth following your dreams. I say this as someone who's dreamed of having a dog since I was four and my parents always said no." I motion toward my smelly disaster, who is on his back while a Labrador bites his throat.

Yeah, he's totally embarrassing me in front of the most attractive person I've ever met, but he's also my source of joy every day, so I can forgive him.

"Thanks for saying that." Ava searches my face, something unreadable passing behind their light brown eyes. "To be honest, when I told my parents I wanted to be an astronaut, they told me to pick something more realistic."

I open my mouth, not sure how to respond.

Ava drops their gaze, and I hope they don't regret confessing that to me.

"You could do it," I say firmly. Even if their parents don't believe in them, I do.

A few strides away, Moose hunches over, and I realize he's taking a crap. He makes eye contact with me.

Okay, nope. Screw the people who told me a dog park is a good place to make friends. This is the most awkward way to meet someone on the entire planet.

I get a poop bag and transfer Moose's gift to the trash can, silently cursing the entire world. Then I return to the ridiculously attractive person who just watched me pick up a mound of dog crap.

"This isn't the way I envisioned meeting a cute person in L.A.," I blurt, needing to get it out there. "I swear my life isn't normally this chaotic."

Ava opens their mouth in surprise before breaking into laughter. "Well, that's dogs."

Pretzel sniffs around calmly, ignoring any dog that tries to engage him. Why can't Moose be chill like that?

"Meg." Ava nudges me playfully and a spark shoots up my arm. "I assure you, you've got my interest."

I open my mouth but nothing comes out.

Really? I do? My pulse accelerates, and I struggle to keep my cool.

We're standing close enough that their sweet lavender scent draws me in again. Their gaze traces over me in a way that makes my insides tingle.

"You're the first stranger I've talked to since moving two weeks ago," I say. "It's hard to make friends in this city."

"I get that. I've lived here my whole life and still have that problem. You have to be bold, I think." Ava looks down at Pretzel, who whines as if saying he's ready to leave.

Bold. There's that word again.

I can do that. I hope.

Across the park, Moose trips over a rock and collides with a golden retriever. I pretend not to notice.

"Hey, I'm having a game night on Friday with a few people, if you're up for some chaos," Ava says in a rush, and if I'm not mistaken, there's a note of nervousness in their voice.

My heart skips. "Really? I'd love to come!"

They grin, their shoulders dropping in relief. "What's your number?"

Friends! I've done it!

And maybe… at some point… more than friends? I bite my lip and type my number in their phone, unable to believe that my ridiculous dog didn't ruin my chance of meeting someone today.

Ava pockets their phone with a sheepish smile. "Cool. Well, I have to get going. Off to my non-exciting, non-astronaut job."

"I guess I'll go give Moose a bath," I say, trying not to betray how disappointed I am that they're leaving already.

"It was nice meeting you." Ava stretches out a hand. "See you here tomorrow?"

"Tomorrow. Yes." I meet their handshake, and as our hands grasp, a pleasant sensation ripples through me.

Their breath hitches, and they bite their lip. With the way their eyes are blazing, I may melt into a puddle right here. I imagine them pulling me in and kissing me passionately, which makes me awkwardly drop my gaze to my feet.

Ava lifts my hand and kisses the back of it, their lips sending a tingle up my arm.

As we let go, they flash a lopsided smile, and I forget how to breathe.

"How bold," I say teasingly.

"Just want to make myself clear," they say with a wink, making my heart flutter.

Pretzel has wandered down to the shoreline, where he and Moose are chasing seagulls. I'm pretty sure the birds are in on the game because they keep landing and casually taking off before the dogs can catch them.

It would be cute, except it's stopping Ava from catching Pretzel.

I run forward to help, grabbing Moose in a weird rodeo move. I get mud all over my jeans but it works, and I use my free hand to hold Pretzel by the collar.

As Ava clips on the leash, our hands brush for longer than necessary.

Damn, there's a serious spark here. The butterflies in my chest are going wild. Should I make my feelings clear too?

"Um, bye then," I say.

Be bold.

And channeling Moose's chaotic energy, throwing any sense of caution and predictability to the wind, seizing the boldness that made me move to L.A. in the first place... I lean in to kiss Ava's cheek.

Without hesitating, Ava turns their head to meet my lips.

A spark of victory ignites in my chest as our lips touch.

The kiss is soft and gentle, and when we pull apart, Ava's lips stretch into a wide smile.

I smile back. "Just wanted to make myself clear," I say, breathless.

Ava laughs. They hold my gaze, a glimmer of excitement in their brown eyes, while Moose and Pretzel wag their tails at the birds in the water.

Until She Kills Me

When enemy spies from opposing agencies come face-to-face, years of tension get resolved.

Outside my apartment, I reach for my pistol, my heart pounding. The gray thread I wedged between the door and the frame is on the floor, which means someone opened the door while I was gone—and yet, my T.A.S.K.-issued security sensor never tripped.

This means that whoever is in my apartment knows what they're doing.

I steel myself with a deep breath, put the key in the lock, and turn it. The deadbolt clicks loudly, spiking my pulse.

There's one explanation for this: the wrong people found out where I live, and they've come to kill me.

Swiftly, I open the door and step inside, pistol up, ready to engage.

Silence. The lights are off like I left them.

In my pocket, my phone buzzes, alerting me about my own feet tripping the sensor.

I leave it. If I don't respond to it within ninety seconds, T.A.S.K. will deploy agents to my place. And I might need their help.

I use my foot to shut the door, then use my elbow to flip on the light.

Everything is as expected—blackout curtains drawn, blanket and pillows in disarray on the couch, mug on the side table, video game controller and toast crumbs on the coffee table.

My buzzing phone fills the space, impeding my ability to hear whoever is here. I remove a hand from my pistol to take the phone out of my pocket and toss it onto the couch.

The hairs on the back of my neck lift. There's a subtle, almost inaudible rustle beside me.

I spin and duck, aiming my weapon at the noise.

She appears in the open doorway to the guest bedroom, her pistol raised. The muzzles of our weapons are an inch apart.

My heart jumps. It's not surprise I feel, but something mixed and confusing. It's more like sudden recognition—like the disarming feeling of spotting someone you know at the grocery store.

Of course it's her.

Nicky looks the same as the last time I saw her two years ago, strong, cool, steady. She still has that unreadable layer beneath the shell she works so hard to uphold. More tattoos than I remember cover her tan skin, peeking out of the sleeves of her black jumpsuit, and she's swapped her fade haircut for an edgier, buzzed look. Her brown eyes are heavier and she looks older than her twenty-four years, leaving me to wonder what kind of assignments she's been on.

"Are you always this tense when you get home?" she asks.

I cock an eyebrow. "You were sloppy."

I lunge for her, thrusting her pistol toward the ceiling so I can bring her to the ground. She reacts with trained speed, blocking my punches and kicks. Her broad shoulders and muscular thighs give her an advantage, but I've always been more nimble.

I grab the lamp beside us and slam it into her gut, winding her. The bulb smashes, and the room darkens. I seize the chance to kick her legs out from under her and get her on her back.

She hits the floor and loses her grip on her pistol.

I point mine at her, panting.

How is it that every time Nicky and I meet, we leave each other bruised and breathless? And not in the fun sense.

My phone stops buzzing. I have ninety seconds.

"Why today, of all days?" I ask. "I've been on a break all month. I was on a date tonight."

From the floor, Nicky's brown eyes trace over me like she's evaluating my choice of high-waisted jeans and a yellow crop top. Yeah, it's a little brighter and cheerier than I usually dress, but I thought it looked hot.

Something crosses Nicky's expression that I can't decipher.

"I don't ask too many questions about my assignments," she says.

I lean closer. "That's the difference between you and me. I like to know what I'm getting into and why. I guess that's why I'm in an intelligence unit and you're just a hired gun."

Her face twists in anger before she regains her composure. "Too bad your *intelligence unit* doesn't care that you've got a target on you."

"So there's a bounty on me?"

"I'm not here to collect a bounty."

I raise an eyebrow. "What, then?"

My heart is pounding, and my patience is wearing thin. There are two ways this can end: either Nicky gets whatever she came for or I kill her. We've crossed paths enough that I intimately know her dedication to the job, and I know she won't leave my apartment until she's completed her assignment.

"They want the Munich files," she says.

Oh. Shit.

I guess this is going to end the second way.

I tighten my finger over the trigger. "Hm. Too bad for them."

Nicky rolls her eyes. "Just get it for me and I'll leave you alone, Ebony."

"I don't have it. I'm serious. If you'd asked questions before agreeing to this assignment, you would have realized that."

She searches my face, clearly trying to decide if I'm lying.

I keep my expression neutral. The flash drive she wants happens to be in the sole of a pair of old boots at the back of the hall closet. She would never find it, even if she had all day to turn my place upside down.

She must realize that, or else I would've come home to a ransacked apartment instead of the end of her pistol.

She grabs a blade from a pocket over her bicep and launches to her feet.

I step back, letting it happen—and as my brain catches up with my reaction, I'm furious with myself. Why didn't I shoot her in the arm to keep her down?

"Are you going to torture me for its whereabouts?" I taunt, cocking an eyebrow. "Come on, make me squeal."

She tilts her head as if considering my offer. "I can just hang out here until you change your mind. Or until you've proven useless."

I scoff. "Let's be honest, Nicky. If we really wanted to, one of us would have killed the other by now. We've both had plenty of opportunities over the last few years. So why haven't you killed me?"

She says nothing.

We're frozen, neither of us making a move. Beyond the windows, traffic whooshes by and people laugh and shout in the street below.

"That's what I thought," I say quietly.

"You thought what, exactly?" she snaps, stepping closer.

"That you can't bring yourself to kill me."

"Oh, please. I wouldn't be where I am today if I was too soft to kill."

"I never said you're soft."

There's a tiny, nondescript beep behind me. Since I haven't addressed the silent alarm, this is the part where T.A.S.K. is listening, waiting for a report through the device on my end table, which looks like an ordinary Bluetooth speaker.

I could say nothing. I could keep talking to Nicky to let them know that I'm in trouble, and they'll send a team to kill her.

Instead, I hold up a hand to Nicky and say, "Hey, guys, I'm fine. I couldn't find my phone."

Nicky's eyes widen, which sends a flash of satisfaction through me.

Yes, honey, you'd be fucked if I'd made a different choice right now.

"Are you serious, Ebony?" Clark asks on the other end, voice tinny.

"Sorry."

"It's fucking midnight. I was asleep."

"I'll make it up to you, man."

"Whatever. Keep your phone on you next time, and don't do it again."

I wait ten seconds, holding Nicky's gaze, letting her process what a mistake she made by breaking into my apartment.

"You're lucky I'm feeling generous tonight," I murmur.

She steps closer until we're a breath apart. "I'll tell my boss you don't have it?"

"Correct."

She extends a hand, and I take it.

The feel of her palm against mine sends a rush through me, like an electric current traveling up my arm and into my chest. The familiar smell of her cologne meets my nose, making my head spin.

"How was your date tonight?" she asks.

"Still thinking about that, huh?"

A flush creeps into her cheeks. I don't think I've ever seen her blush before.

"It was terrible," I admit. "She was clearly not over her ex."

"Sorry to hear that."

"No you're not."

Her mouth opens in surprise. She struggles for words, can't seem to find any, and closes her mouth again.

We haven't let go of each other's hand.

As much as I want to hate her, to accept that we are supposed to be enemies, to do my job and just kill her... there's a competing pull inside me. I can't forget the years we spent in training, all of those days and nights we spent getting to know each other. She was my best friend and my anchor. If it weren't for her, I don't know if I would've had the emotional strength to make it through training.

"Nicky, do you ever wonder what would've happened if we hadn't been separated—"

"Every day," she says, and she's close enough that her breath tickles my face.

The thing I've wondered all these years burns hotter than ever inside me. What would have happened if T.A.S.K. hired both of us? Would we have acted on our feelings? If we worked for the same agency, we could have been a team, and I could rely on her strength instead of battling it.

Instead we're here, destined to fight, poised to kill each other.

But if we aren't allowed to have a life together... if we aren't allowed a future... maybe we could have just one night. After all the work I've done for T.A.S.K., and all of my unwavering loyalty, don't I deserve it?

"I volunteered for this assignment, Ebony," Nicky says, the words seeming to spill out. "I wanted to see you."

I don't know what to say to this, so I say nothing. Is this all we get? We can only see each other if we've each got a gun in our hand?

She steps closer. "I don't regret getting hired by a different agency than you. But what I do regret is not acting on my feelings before we were separated."

My breath catches. My heart slams into my ribs, the truth painful to hear. "Your feelings?"

She gives a tiny, almost imperceptible nod.

We're standing so close that I feel her breath on my face. My knees weaken, and for a moment, I feel like someone other than an agent—just a woman with a crush.

"Nicky…" I whisper, moving my hand so our fingers interlock.

I want to kiss her. Is that a terrible idea? Should we part ways before we do something we'll regret?

Whatever Nicky sees in my eyes makes her fingers tighten over mine. With a fiery, blazing look, she pulls me all the way in.

Our lips meet in a kiss that should have happened years ago. I hold her face in my hands, then slide them around the back of her neck. She grips my waist, holding me close. She's rough and gentle at the same time, claiming me while making sure not to hurt me. She's always been like this—hard on the outside, but secretly soft and vulnerable. I've never forgotten the way she used to break down to me after a bad day of training, making me swear not to tell a soul about her weakness.

I never considered her emotions a weakness. To me, she was just human, and it made me fall hard for her.

Our kiss deepens, our hands moving faster over each other's bodies, like we're making up for lost time.

She walks me back, and I stumble as we head toward the couch. Her arms tighten around me, holding me to her.

We fall onto the couch, and she's on top of me, her breath warm on my neck. Her pistol slides to the floor with a *thump* and I place mine on the coffee table with a trembling hand.

I moan, wrapping my legs around her to pin her to me.

"What if we could change things?" I ask.

She hesitates.

I run my hands over her breasts, down her waist, and between her legs. She hisses as my hand rubs a slow circle outside her jumpsuit.

"It's too late," she whispers. "You think they'll believe that one of us has suddenly changed her allegiance? You think it's safe to tell them that?"

With fumbling hands, she unbuttons my jeans, and I help her take them off before turning my attention to her jumpsuit.

We lock lips, grabbing each other, shedding our clothes frantically. Then we're naked, and the weight of her body on mine leaves me dizzy. She's strong and chiseled, and yet her skin is achingly soft. I'm burning everywhere we're touching—breasts, stomach, thighs.

She reaches between my legs and rubs, and I close my eyes, sinking into how good she feels. Goosebumps ripple across my body.

I pull her mouth to mine, nipping and sucking her lip, arching my back to get closer.

"Would you ever think about quitting?" she whispers into my mouth.

I don't answer, which makes her pull back.

"No?" she says.

"Not quitting. But that doesn't mean I don't regret where we both ended up."

"Hm."

Her fingers massage me faster, making me gasp. I reach down to do the same to her, and she moans into my mouth.

We rock against each other, kissing hard.

I run my fingers over her short hair and grip the back of her neck. "I—I think T.A.S.K. would hire you," I say, finding it harder to get the words out.

"They wouldn't."

"We could use a double agent."

She pauses, leaving me wet and panting. I grab her hand and make her keep going, aching for her.

"Maybe," she whispers, but I hear the doubt in her tone. I see it in her eyes. She won't risk it.

I slide a finger into her, making her gasp. Her legs tremble.

"E, you feel so good," she whispers.

My insides flutter at her use of the nickname. She hasn't called me E in years.

"So do you," I murmur.

I pull her mouth back to mine. Like everything that happens between us, I'm torn between feeling in control and totally powerless. I'm exposed beneath her, naked and pinned to the couch, her fingers making me tremble and lose control.

But I've got her the same way, gasping, begging, totally vulnerable.

Maybe that's the way it's meant to be between us—an eternal power struggle, a mess of feelings that never get resolved.

As we get lost in each other, I let myself dream of a world where we weren't separated in the academy. One where we weren't forced to be enemies. One where we were allowed to tell each other how we felt without fear of punishment.

An alternate world.

Anywhere but here and now.

Because in this world, this night is all we get.

Nicky crawls lower, kissing my chest, stomach, and hips. Between my legs, she moves her tongue in a way that makes me gasp.

God, she makes it hard for me to do what needs to be done.

It was a mistake for her to come here. She knows where I live, and I know she sees through my lie. She knows I have the Munich files.

As long as she's alive and working against me, national security will be compromised. Which gives me two choices.

I could go off the grid and run away with her, leaving behind everything I've worked for...

Or I can kill her and end our eternal power struggle.

Her tongue moves faster, and I cry out, sinking into the couch.

I can't care about her. I can't lose everything I've worked for.

Breathing hard, dizzy with pleasure, I turn my head to look at the coffee table, where my pistol is waiting to be fired.

The Knight and Her Princess

A knight in shining armor rescues a princess from a tower, and their feelings from the past can no longer be ignored.

Galloping hooves and clanking armor fill my ears as I charge toward the dark fortress, one of twenty Knights of East Abria. Purpose floods my veins, sharpening my senses and readying my muscles for a fight.

Men shout and roar around me. Swords glint in the sunlight. As we roll over the grassy hillside like a storm, it's clear why we are considered the most powerful force in the eight realms.

Except I'm struggling to stay in the saddle, wheezing for breath as my chestnut mare throws a fit beneath me.

Catching up on his bay stallion, Sir Athdar laughs heartily. "Brianna, darling, part of becoming a knight is learning how to ride."

"It's Dame Brianna," I shout, pulling the reins. "And I'll gladly trade you for your pussycat of a stallion."

God Almighty. If I make it home, I'm going to have a word with the stable master. This mare is barely broke to ride and has the personality of cursed fire.

Queen Augusta's castle looms ahead, its stone towers brighter than those back home, with ivy and flowers blanketing the sides. I hate to call it lovely, given that these towers are imprisoning our princess, but it truly is.

With a groan, I use all my strength to keep my mare's head up and stop her from bucking. Finally, she gives up the fight and surges forward. Satisfaction pulls my lips into a grin as we pick up speed.

"See you at the tower," I shout over my shoulder, and we pull ahead of Sir Athdar, the mare's hooves chewing up the grass.

After fighting hard to earn my place as a knight, I'd naively hoped the others would accept my achievement. But my journey to knighthood was only the beginning of my battle.

I should have known this struggle would stay with me for life. Only three women before me have ever been knighted, and two were accepted because they were noble-born. The other was accepted because her twin brother was a knight, and the royals saw it as a good omen.

As for me? I'm here on skill alone.

My build has never served me. I'm too tall, too muscular, and according to most men, not feminine enough in any sense of the word. But I was born for knighthood. I've imagined it since I watched a joust at six years old, and now, as I cross the plains on my first mission with the wind stinging my cheeks, my heart fills with victory.

I just hope I can prove that I deserve the title.

My fiery mare gets me to the drawbridge first. Queen Augusta's guards see us and rush to raise it—but the mole we sent yesterday did his job well. The chains are cut, and the bridge will not rise.

"Charge!" Sir Athdar calls, taking the word from my mouth.

We storm across in a clatter of hooves, meeting Queen Augusta's guards with our swords swinging.

The knights around me dive into the fight, swarming the courtyard, roaring and whooping like they've waited a lifetime for this.

My thoughts are in one place: the tower on the right with the butterfly-shaped stone on the side. That's where the Green Witch said Princess Enid is trapped.

"Check all of the towers!" Sir Athdar shouts, directing the other knights with the tip of his sword.

"It's this one!" I shout, pointing to the one on the right.

"So the crone said. She could be wrong."

I grit my teeth. He might not trust the Green Witch, but she has served East Abria for a hundred years, and her word is our best shot.

I steer my mount through the crowd, aiming for the tower with the butterfly-shaped stone. The mare responds eagerly, as keen as I am to get away from the clashing swords and bloodshed.

We skid to a stop at the wooden door, and I leap from the saddle.

"See what happens when we work together?" I say to the mare, who snorts and tosses her head.

I attack the wooden door with my ax, grunting with the effort.

Please be the right tower. We don't have time to blunder around the castle. We have one chance, and if the Green Witch's vision was wrong, we might all die before we find Princess Enid.

Sir Athdar reins to a stop beside me and dismounts. "If you're so stubborn, then."

"I owe you a flagon of mead if I'm wrong."

With a few swings, we crash through the door. I stumble into the dark tower, regaining my balance with considerable effort as my armor tries to weigh me down.

As I'm the first one inside, Sir Athdar pushes me onward, readying his sword and shield. "Go, Brianna! We'll hold them off."

"It's Dame Brianna!" I race up the spiral stairs, my heavy armor making me lose my breath rapidly.

I pass door after door, trusting the witch's instructions. *The top. She's at the very top.*

I trip in the darkness, unable to see a bloody thing through my helmet. I remove it and set it in a nook for later, then push my short, dark locks off my sweaty forehead and keep going.

Finally, the stone steps end, and I come to another wooden door.

Wheezing for breath, I raise my ax. "Princess Enid?"

"Go away!" a muffled voice shouts from the other side.

My heart leaps. We've done it. That tone is definitely hers.

I set to work on the hinges, gasping for breath between swings. Sweat rolls down my back, dampening my tunic.

The hinges crack, and I kick the door down.

"Princess?"

An unmade bed sits in the middle of the circular room, covered in jewels of every color. Tapestries, furniture, and bookshelves fill the space, as extravagant as I would expect from Queen Augusta.

Princess Enid stands against the far wall, illuminated by a beam of sunlight coming through the window. My chest flutters at the sight of her, tall and mature in a green gown. Her pale skin is dusted in freckles, just like I remember.

"Leave at once!" she says fiercely, holding up her fists.

I'm frozen in place.

The last time we saw each other, we were hardly fourteen. Now, she's an eighteen-year-old beauty, her face full, her waist curved, her curly red hair well-groomed. Her familiar features pull my memories forward, making my insides tingle—her soft skin beneath my palms, her lips against mine, the rush of something forbidden coursing through me. How often did we escape to the stables during that year together? Fifty, sixty, a hundred times?

Heat rises in my face. God, I thought my feelings had dissolved. With years to forget her, and knighthood to draw my focus, I'd hoped she could become my past and nothing more.

Seeing her now, I'm weak in the knees, and I know I failed to forget about her.

Remembering my duty, I dip into a bow. "Princess Enid, I have ridden here with the Knights of East Abria to rescue you and return you to your realm."

Princess Enid gapes at me.

Far below, the clamor of battle rings out. I sheath my ax and place a hand on the hilt of my sword.

Hold them off, Sir Athdar. We'll be out soon.

"Have you not heard me? I don't want you here," the princess finally says, scowling. She marches toward me, her hands up like she's ready to shove me out the door.

My insides seem to hollow out. She doesn't recognize me.

Well, it will be easier this way. I can do my job and bring her safely—

"Brianna?" she says, stopping with a hand on her chest.

My heart skips. "Yes. Hi."

She's frozen, taking me in with wide eyes. "You're a knight!"

I look down at myself as if to check whether her words are true. The sight of my armor makes me stand taller. "Yes."

"But I—I thought your father was going to make you marry that tailor."

I almost smile. "Princess, do you honestly think I would have given myself over to a man?"

She flushes, possibly remembering how many times I proved to her that I wasn't interested in men.

"Brianna!" Sir Athdar shouts far below. "Have you found her? Hurry!"

"I can store your belongings in my satchel while we ride back," I say, turning our attention to the jewels on the bed. "Your father will be disappointed if we leave them behind."

"Um—right," Princess Enid says, scooping them into a pile. She shoves her tiara through her red curls, where it sits lopsided, and tosses the jewels into my open satchel.

We're standing so close that I can count the freckles dusting her nose and cheeks. Her eyes are as blue as cornflowers. Did I really think I could forget how beautiful she is? Or was I denying it all these years to make the pain of being apart hurt less?

"I suppose I should call you Dame Brianna, then," she says, her breath warm and sweet on my face.

"To you, I'm still just Brianna."

She smiles. "The armor looks good on you."

"My parents say they would prefer me in a gown."

"I don't." She searches my face with her piercing eyes, her brow pinched. "Brianna, I never stopped wondering what happened to—"

"Don't. We knew it would end one day."

Her breath catches, and she looks so sad that I want nothing more than to step in and hold her. "I never wanted it to," she whispers.

I swallow hard. It's bittersweet to hear these words. "Nor did I. But you're a princess. I'm nobody."

"You're not nobody! You never were."

"Darling, you know a Princess and a common girl would never have been allowed. For more than one reason."

"So all of our time together was a waste?" she asks, her voice thick.

I step closer. "No! Never a waste. My time with you was the best of my life. And in truth—" I swallow hard. "In truth, I trained to become a knight because you inspired me to be more. I always dreamed of it, but you were the one who made me believe I could do it."

Her breath catches. She looks out of place in this dark room, like a vision illuminated in the beam of sunlight. "Brianna, I have to tell you, I—"

Footsteps thump on the stairs.

I push Princess Enid behind me and draw my sword. "Who's there?"

Sir Athdar rushes in, wheezing. "Thank goodness we found her. Come on, Princess."

He strides over and scoops her into his arms, eliciting cries from both of us.

"I don't need to be carried!" Princess Enid shouts.

"Sir Athdar, please," I say, putting a hand on his arm.

"There is no time," he says, rushing down the spiral stairs with the princess struggling in his arms. "Brianna, gather what's left of our stolen possessions and follow me. We won't be able to hold them off much longer."

"I am not a possession!" Princess Enid shouts, punching him everywhere she can manage.

I hesitate, then shove any remaining jewels and clothes into my satchel before racing after them.

Crashes and shouts rise from the bottom of the tower, and Sir Athdar stops. Princess Enid stops struggling. I cover my mouth, silencing my breaths.

"Sir Athdar," someone shouts, "they've broken our circle."

He curses. Princess Enid takes the opportunity to writhe free of his arms. She lands clumsily on her feet and straightens up, glowering.

"Sir, I will bring the princess down with me," I whisper.

"And I am capable of walking down stairs myself!" Princess Enid snaps at him.

Sir Athdar looks between us. "Fine. If you let her get hurt, it's on you, Brianna."

With a final glare, he rushes down the steps to help the others.

The moment he's out of sight, Princess Enid's hand clasps mine, so small and delicate through my stiff leather glove.

"Brianna," she whispers.

I'm a step below her, looking up into her beautiful eyes. "I promise we'll get you home, Princ—"

"Shh." She leans in, and as her sweet breath tickles my face, my heart skips.

My mouth is dry. It's hard to say what needs to be said. "Darling, I want to, but we shouldn't—"

Her lips press against mine, silencing me, and her hands link around the back of my neck. She pulls herself closer to me, and all thoughts of what we should and shouldn't do dissolve.

Oh, God, Enid's kiss is enough to tip me off balance. I desperately want to be rid of this armor so I can feel her soft curves against my skin.

She traces her fingers up the back of my neck and through my hair, which is a lot shorter than when I last saw her. She doesn't seem to mind.

The kiss brings forth everything I remember about her. I thought I'd forgotten what she tasted like, the way her lips moved, the little sounds she made—but it all comes back in a rush that leaves me breathless.

I lift my hands to her hair, running them through her curls.

Her lips part, and our kiss deepens. She cups her soft, cool hands on my cheeks, the only part of me that isn't hidden by armor.

I run my fingers down her bodice, and her breath hitches. The sound stirs something in me, making me want to carry her back up the stairs and lay her on the bed. I trace my fingers over her chest, hooking them over her dress where the tops of her breasts are teasing me.

This is torture. She's a woman now—we both are, and we've had years to think about each other and grow bolder in what we want. And oh, the things I want to do right now. I want to see every inch of her, feel her, taste her…

Below, Sir Athdar shouts, "Brianna, all clear! Let's go!"

Princess Enid and I pull apart. Her lips are full from the kiss, her cheeks flushed.

"Come on," I whisper. I hold her hand, pulling her gently down the steps with me.

She resists. "Brianna, I…" She swallows hard. "I don't want to be rescued."

I blink, and the words hover between us before I can speak. "What do you mean?"

"I came here of my own accord. Queen Augusta is my aunt, and she is the only one who understands."

"Understands *what*?" I squeeze her hands, wishing my gloves weren't between us. "Why would you come live in this tower, away from everyone you love?"

"Because I'm eighteen and my father expects me to marry. If I live under Queen Augusta's rule, she won't make me. Brianna, she is married to a *lady*. The witches blessed her vows to Lady Moira."

I open my mouth, understanding crashing over me. "Oh."

I avoided becoming some man's wife by training to be a knight. But Princess Enid didn't have that option. She was left with a choice: marry a man and produce an heir, or run away.

We stare at each other. My pulse quickens as I realize I need to make a decision.

"Do you want me to leave you?" I ask, a tremor in my voice.

"No," she says quickly, holding my hands tighter. "I want—"

Below, someone shouts for us to hurry.

"I'll go after them," Sir Athdar says.

"We're coming!" I shout. I lean closer to Princess Enid. "Princess, tell me what you want me to do."

Her eyes brim with tears. "I don't know. The knights won't let me stay here, no matter how much I protest or try to hide from them. My father sent them, so they'll drag me home."

"*I* won't drag you home," I say fiercely. But despite my strong words, a shiver runs through me. What am I supposed to do? I can't leave her here because the king won't allow it. I'm a knight, and bringing her home is my duty.

But I don't want to force her to come home if she doesn't want to.

I study the stone floor as if hoping to find the answer there. My heart leaps against my ribs as a possibility stretches out in my mind. "Is Queen Augusta in need of another knight?"

Princess Enid's expression goes blank. "What do you mean?"

"I mean—" I draw a shaky breath. "If I stayed here with you, could I be a knight in her service? In *your* service?"

It's a dangerous proposal—treason, even. But my heart is speaking stronger words than my mind, and my loyalty has always been to Princess Enid more than anyone else. If she is here in Queen Augusta's realm, then I want to be here with her.

Princess Enid stands taller, her face brightening, and I don't think I have ever seen her smile so widely. She throws her arms around my neck, kissing me hard. "Yes! Yes!" she says between kisses.

A rush of pleasure surges through me. I wrap my arms around her waist, holding her close. "Yes?"

"I know she will accept you as she accepted me. And I want you here more than I have ever wanted anything. Oh, Brianna…" She takes my hand and pulls me up the stairs, her face alight.

"But the knights," I say, my head swimming. "They're all fighting down below!"

"We'll go to Queen Augusta straight away. Come quickly."

She pulls me to one of the doors I ran past on the way up, and pushes it open. Beyond it is a long hallway leading to the rest of the castle—to a new life, a new queen, and a future with Princess Enid.

All I need to do is walk down it.

"Are—are you sure she'll have me?" I say, swallowing hard.

Princess Enid kisses me, sending a tendril of heat through my midsection. "Dame Brianna," she whispers, "you came here to rescue me, and you are the only one who is listening to what I want. You are, I believe, the noblest of all knights. I *know* she'll have you."

This is reckless, hasty, not planned whatsoever... but I have to try. I won't force Enid to come back with me, and I can't imagine leaving her behind and spending the rest of my life without her. If she's here, then I must do whatever it takes to be here with her.

A flame of excitement ignites in my chest. I hold her hands firmly in mine. "All right, Princess. I trust you."

"And you're certain you will be happy here?" she asks, searching my face with her brilliant blue eyes.

I smile. "Enid, darling, if I am allowed to spend my whole life serving you, I swear I will be the happiest knight in the world."

Bonus: The Princess's Bed Chambers

One year later, Brianna and Enid share an intimate moment in the midst of a busy day.

I knock on the golden door of Enid's chambers, a flutter of nerves in my chest. "Darling, can I come in?"

Footsteps rush closer and the door flies open. She's in a breathtaking blue gown that complements her eyes, and her curly red hair is in a thick plait. With flushed cheeks and a wide smile, she grabs my hand. "There you are! Where have you been all morning?"

"I had matters to—" Before I can finish, Enid pulls me into a firm kiss, and kicks the door shut.

"I've decided I'm going to ask Queen Augusta if you can sleep in my chambers with me," she whispers into my lips. "It's ridiculous. We're both of age, and—"

"Don't you dare," I say, pulling back.

"Why not?" She pushes her bottom lip out, looking adorable.

"Asking the queen if we can share a bed out of wedlock? I think I'll die of embarrassment." I kiss her pouting lips before she can raise another protest. "I've just seen her, actually, and she wants to speak with you. She's waiting in the garden."

"Mm," Enid says, wrapping her arms around my neck and pulling me into a deeper kiss. She presses her body closer, and the feel of her breasts and hips against me are enough to make me melt into her. The material of her gown is blissfully thin, leaving nothing to my imagination.

"Enid," I say, losing my breath. "Did you hear me? The queen wants—"

"She can wait," she murmurs into my mouth.

I would laugh at the absurdity of making the queen wait, but Enid's hand is under my tunic, teasing the waistband of my riding trousers. Heat builds inside me.

"You—are always so defiant," I say, gasping.

"And that's what you love about me."

I grip the curve of her waist, holding her close. My thoughts are scattering, all sense of urgency disappearing as her hand slips inside my trousers. She glides it between my legs, and I moan, tightening my grip on her.

"Oh, you sly…" It's hard to speak as she moves her fingers back and forth. The sensation makes me shiver.

I close my eyes, kissing her slowly, lost in the sweet taste of her lips. I circle my palms over her breasts, where I can feel her hard nipples through the material.

Her fingers move faster. My insides are already aching for a release.

"Okay, you win," I growl. "I've forgotten why I came here."

She lets out a delighted laugh as I spin us around and push her up against the wall. She flattens a tapestry of a woman among some roses.

The room the queen gave Enid is absurdly nicer than mine, but with our difference in status, I would expect no less. Where my chambers are full of practical furniture made of wood, stone, and wool, hers are full of art and extravagances—gold, silver, silk.

Enid is flushed, breathing fast, her plait coming undone as I hold her against the wall and kiss her everywhere. I leave a trail of kisses on her neck, chest, and arms, and then crouch so I can move lower.

"Oh, Brianna…" I love the way my name sounds like a melody coming from her lips.

On my knees, I lift her gown and pull down her undergarments. "Hold this," I say, guiding her delicate hands to hold the skirt out of the way.

"Okay," she whispers, and the moment her hands are around the hem of her dress, I lean in.

I lick between her legs, and she makes a noise like a stifled scream.

I use my fingers to part her, then lick her again. I go slowly, teasing her, until she trembles.

The taste of her is a familiar comfort, something I've cherished since the first time we kissed in the stables years ago—and something I plan to never live without.

"I love you so much," I whisper.

"I love you too," she says, stammering, sinking lower against the wall as pleasure overtakes her.

Needing more of her, I place a hand under her thigh and lift it up.

She gasps. "Oh, God."

I move my tongue faster, exploring her, losing myself like I have so many times before. My insides burn, a flame igniting in me and dancing between us. Enid whimpers, swaying.

I recognize the shifting rhythm of her breath, the way her skin ripples with gooseflesh, and the increasing dampness between her legs. She's losing control, and it won't take much more.

I hold her firmly and move my tongue faster, and she moans louder, and when I change my rhythm to just the way she likes it, she cries out. Her knees buckle. I hold her tight as waves of pleasure cascade over her, leaving her breathless.

When she stops and gasps for air, I pull her gently down to the floor with me. We kiss, and I let her catch her breath in my arms.

"That was a wonderful distraction," I murmur into her hair. "And we really do need to go down to the gardens now."

She laughs. "But what about your turn?"

"Later," I say with a wink. As much as I want to stay here for another hour, we have somewhere important to be.

We stay on the floor for another moment while Enid recovers, then we clean up and fix our hair and clothes so it isn't so obvious what we were doing.

As we head outside hand-in-hand, Enid leans in and whispers in my ear, "I'm going to exercise my tongue on you the moment we're done here."

I grin, tingling between my legs. This, I can agree to. "Well, if you insist…"

We walk to the garden we've spent endless hours in. It's the most beautiful spot in Queen Augusta's realm, full of every type of flower, bird, and butterfly imaginable—a symphony to the eyes, ears, and nose.

As we duck beneath the arbor and enter the garden, Enid sees what's there and stops in her tracks.

Queen Augusta isn't here. Of course she isn't, because that was a lie. I told Enid that just to get her down here. Though it nearly didn't work.

Always so defiant…

Silver draperies guide us to a point, where pink and red rose petals cover the ground. I tug her by the hand, taking her to the center of the garden.

"Brianna, what..." Enid turns to face me, her cornflower blue eyes wide with wonder.

Heart hammering against my ribs, my face breaks into an uncontrollable smile.

Enid lets out a little scream as I pull the ring from my pocket and get down on one knee.

Just a Rebound

Claire goes out for a night of clubbing with a casual fling in mind… but when she meets Lou, priorities change.

"I'm just saying, my favorite part of clubbing is normally the part where I go home and crawl into bed," I shout in Michelle's ear, grimacing at the sight of the writhing bodies on the dance floor. I don't recognize this awful bass-heavy song, and it smells like spilled alcohol and sweat in here.

"Oh, shut up," Michelle says, shoving me. "This was your idea, Claire."

"Life is full of regrets." I squirm in my black dress, which is so tiny that I'm having a hard time keeping my butt and nipples covered at the same time.

It's nearly midnight, and I'm normally in bed by now. I wistfully imagine putting on PJs, scrubbing off my makeup, and sliding between the sheets in the cool silence of my apartment.

But I did have a goal for tonight, and I should stick this out, right? After that dumpster fire of a breakup last week, it would be healthy and invigorating if this night would end with me naked in someone else's bed. I want to feel wanted, even if it's just a fling.

"Chad, eleven o'clock," Michelle shouts in my ear as we push through the crowd toward the dance floor.

It's hard to miss the guy she's talking about. He's built like an athlete, his chest and arms straining his black V-neck tee. His neck is as thick as his bicep. Based on his blank expression, he also looks like he has the IQ of a potato.

"Maybe," I say, my tone wavering. I did specify that I was after a one-night stand, not a relationship, but something about him isn't doing it for me.

"No gym guys? Do you want an intellect instead?" Michelle pulls me to the left. "Here, business major, straight ahead."

Beyond a squealing bachelorette party, there's a guy in a suit. I'm not sure if that means he's an intellectual or just trying to give off that vibe.

"I don't know." I cross my arms. "None of them are sparking anything."

Yeah, I'm being difficult, but I'm not sure what I want, and I'm not sure who here will want me back. Something about being among all of these single men is making my skin prickle with nervous sweat.

"That's fine," Michelle says brightly. "That's normal after what you've been through. Do you want a shot?"

Bless Michelle and her undying support.

My expression must say "yes" because she takes my hand and pulls me toward the bar. She's dressed like a bombshell with bright red lipstick to match her red dress, her straight dark hair glinting in the light. I guess I look good too, but I rarely wear dresses, and I'm compulsively touching my chest to make sure a boob hasn't popped out. My stilettos also aren't going well today, and I've nearly twisted my ankle several times. At least my curls are cooperating and the brunette box dye turned out nice.

Michelle orders us tequila, and we shoot it back. We pre-gamed for three hours while we got ready, so I'm already buzzed.

While Michelle pays, I rub my forehead, careful not to smudge my makeup. Why is it so hard to be here right now? Shouldn't I be ready to rebound after a week of sulking over Curtis?

I guess I miss him more than I thought—which is infuriating because he broke up with me the day before Valentine's Day. Who does that?

Ugh, men.

Maybe that's my problem tonight. I'm here looking at men but I've got too many bad feelings about the last one I let into my life. I'm expecting them to be like him, douchey attitude and all.

"We should've gone to Cellar," I admit, thinking longingly of the club full of queer people three blocks away. "I don't think I want to be with a guy tonight."

"Okay," Michelle says with enthusiasm. "The night is young. Wait here, and I'll get our coats."

I crack a smile. "Have I told you I love you?"

"Love you too, bitch."

She disappears into the crowd.

Two people from the loud bachelorette party step up to take her place at the bar, and I move over to give them room.

"You owe me something strong," one says. "I can't believe I just watched male strippers. That's forever in my brain now. Burned. Seared. Tattooed on the back of my eyeballs."

"Don't lie," the other says, a blonde in a pink sash. "I saw you smiling."

"That was probably the moment I remembered we were going for donuts after."

"Can you at least appreciate it as an art form?"

I'm laughing. I can't help it.

The upset one turns around to face me, and—*oh my.* My heart does several backflips.

"I bet this girl agrees," the blonde says, seeing me look over. "Tell my friend Lou they're being ridiculous, and strip shows are an art form."

"Mm, I think I'd find it unbearably awkward to watch and would hate every second of it," I say, and the one named Lou grins.

The blonde scoffs, and turns her attention to waving down the bartender.

I can't help staring. Lou is breathtaking, with light brown skin, dark hair styled in a thick pompadour, a strong jawline and razor-sharp cheekbones, and bold eyeliner. They're in a white button-down shirt that reveals a peek of cleavage, a loose black tie, open blazer, tight trousers, and loafers. It's an unconventional fashion statement for a bachelorette party, and *hot damn*.

"I'm Claire, she/her," I say, melting under the heat of their smolder. "And I'm sorry for your suffering. I would've died being forced to watch a strip show."

They lean against the bar, getting closer. "Lou, they/them. And thank you. There was some helicoptering, and now I have to get fall-down drunk to erase it from my memory."

I don't even cringe at the helicopter thing because I'm so busy trying not to swoon over the sheer amount of confidence oozing from Lou.

Maybe I was too quick to say we should leave this club. If there is even the remotest chance of tonight ending with Lou on top of me, then we are definitely staying.

I'm about to ask how the bachelorette party's going when the blonde waves her phone in Lou's face. "Rebecca just texted and said they're doing a group photo. Come on."

Crap. This might be a little harder than I anticipated.

Lou looks at the ceiling. After enduring several bachelorette parties in my life, I feel their pain so hard. I wonder if the group forces Lou to wear a sash for photos.

"Cool," they say valiantly. "But I want my drink first."

"Oh ya," the blonde says, like she forgot why they were at the bar. She turns back to the bartender and shouts her drink order.

"So who's getting married?" I say, snagging Lou's attention while I have the chance.

"My sister. I'm her Best Man. I mean, Maid of Honor, technically, but she knows me well enough not to use those words."

"Wait, so *you* planned this evening?"

Lou cringes. "Penises, party games, limo, the works. And now here I am in a straight club when my friends are partying at Cellar without me, so..." They give a thumbs-up.

"Wow. Best Man of the year."

"Right? Sis is lucky I love her."

On Lou's other side, Michelle squeezes through the crowd, coming back with our coats. She sees Lou talking to me and stops, her eyes lighting up.

I try to keep a neutral expression as she points from Lou to me with her mouth open.

I nod a little, and she fist-pumps and backs away.

Lou glances back. "Friend?"

"Yeah. She's my wingman tonight."

"And how's that going?"

I lift a shoulder, not sure how to answer. The uncertainty from earlier comes back—not feeling hot enough, not feeling wanted, not sure if going out tonight was the right call.

Lou shifts, brushing against me in the dense crowd. My stomach swoops at the contact.

"What are you looking for?" they say.

You, I think, blushing. "I'm just here to have fun. Getting over a breakup and wanting to do something wild."

I meant it as an invitation to do something wild with me, but Lou gives me a pitying look. "Damn. Sorry to hear—"

"Oh my God, look at Frankie!" the blonde squeals, slapping Lou's arm and pointing across the bar, where the other bridesmaids are obviously doing something rowdy.

Lou glances over, gives a two-note laugh, and then looks back at me.

"I mean, it's fine, we should've broken up months ago but kept clinging to each other," I say to Lou, desperately trying to keep our conversation going. "I guess he and I both thought we were going through a rough patch."

"Ah, been there. You keep fighting, then apologizing without really meaning it, then having aggressive sex to make up…" The blonde passes Lou a drink, and the pause is just long enough for the words *aggressive sex* to loop in my mind. "…then you wake up the next day, and the tiniest thing gets you angry, and you pick up the fight where you left off."

"Pretty much," I say.

The blonde is paying for their drinks, and I have seconds left with Lou. Dammit, I have definitely not put my best foot forward. I wasted precious seconds talking about my breakup with a guy. Am I acting desperate and sad? Is this dress too hetero for Lou to have any clue that I'm queer?

I scramble for something flirty to say. Do I lean against them? Touch their arm? How does one make a "come hither" look, anyway?

"Well, it sounds like you do need a wild time tonight," Lou says, lifting their drink and turning away. "Have fun! It was nice meeting you."

Fuck.

I can't believe I talked about being here for a rebound. What's wrong with me? Lou is clearly worth more than that and doesn't have time to entertain a mess of a human.

"Wait," I say.

They turn back to me, and I don't know what to say next.

Heat rises in my face.

"What—what kind of drink did your friend get you?" I ask, scrambling.

They sip it, contemplating. "I think it's a Long Island Iced Tea."

"Cool."

"Cool. Time to get smashed." Lou lifts their glass in a toast, then turns and disappears through the crowd.

Yep, I'm a hopeless idiot.

Slumping, I find Michelle and tell her about my failure to snag the hottest person in the entire bar. She cheers me up with another tequila shot.

"Probably not the best night for them to hook up, anyway," she says sympathetically. "They'll be too busy with the party."

"I guess. Should we go?"

Michelle hesitates. I'm about to ask what's up when the song changes to *Single Ladies*, and she grabs my hand. "Nope. This is a sign that we need to stay. Come on."

I unstick my feet from the floor, where someone must have spilled a drink. "Fine. Where's Chad at?"

We check our coats again and then dance for two hours, getting drunker by the minute. At some point, I grind on the intellectual guy, and then casually ghost him before he thinks I'm too interested. I avoid Lou out of embarrassment, keeping tabs on where the rowdy bridesmaids are.

Somewhere around two in the morning, I stumble into the bathroom and stand by the sinks to wait for a vacant stall. It's a graffiti-covered disaster in here, and two of the four stalls have no doors. This doesn't stop the women ahead of me from using them while their friends stand in front as human shields.

The bathroom door swings open, letting in the ear-splitting noise of the music and crowd.

Lou walks in.

My heart skips a beat.

I'm trapped. And blushing.

"Claire," they say in mock seriousness. "We meet again."

"Lou. Did the Long Island Iced Tea do its job?"

"Well, I feel like this bathroom is at a fifty degree angle, and I just danced to *Save A Horse, Ride A Cowboy*. So I'd say yep."

I laugh.

We're both sweaty and disheveled from dancing. Their gaze is unfocused, and I'm leaning against the wall for support.

"Hey, I'm sorry I dumped my breakup on you earlier," I say, my tongue moving faster than my brain. "That was not very flirty of me."

They laugh, searching my face with a bit of confusion in their brown eyes. "Flirty?"

A woman walks in behind Lou, and sighs dramatically when she sees the small lineup. She pulls out her phone and starts typing, her long nails clicking loudly.

"Yeah," I say. "Like, I should have batted my eyelashes and touched your arm or something."

Lou says nothing, staring at me.

Someone comes out of a bathroom stall—one with a door—and I head for it.

Before I can shut the door, Lou races up behind me and puts their hand on it, stopping me. Their eyes are wide, their jaw slack. "Wait. When you say *flirty*—are you —interested in me?"

Am I interested? *Babe,* I want to say, *I'd lick you up and down like you're a soft serve ice cream cone and I'm standing under a heat lamp.*

"Well, yeah," I say instead, heat rising in my cheeks.

"I didn't…" Lou checks me out, their dark eyes flicking over my little black dress.

"Didn't realize it because I don't know how to flirt and am dressed like a Kinsey One. I know. I'm not really bringing my A-game tonight."

They give me a devastating half-smile.

My brain is sluggish. Somewhere deep down, it dawns on me that I've solved my earlier problem: Lou now knows I'm interested because I flat-out just said it.

Hm. There's something to be said for being direct.

I sway, grabbing the stall door for support. Well, Michelle succeeded at getting me drunk tonight. I'm feeling pretty good, even if I'm not getting laid.

The impatient woman with the clicky nails clears her throat. "Hey, are you gonna pee or just stand there?"

"Sorry," Lou and I both murmur.

Lou drops their arm but doesn't move, still staring at me. What are they thinking that has them looking at me like this?

If they weren't interested, they would have backed away awkwardly by now, right?

Before the impatient woman can snap at us again, I grab Lou by the tie and pull them into the stall with me.

Their breath hitches, and when I reach around to lock the door, we're nose-to-nose. They're a couple of inches taller than me. I meet their blazing hot gaze through my lashes.

"What do you think?" I whisper.

I really hope I'm not misreading their expression.

"I think…" Lou gives me a charming smile. "I'm blown away that the most beautiful girl in the bar is into me. And I think this bachelorette party just got a lot more interesting."

My heart flips. Lou thinks I'm beautiful? Before I can say anything more, their arms wrap around me, and I incline my head to meet their lips.

They push me against the wall of the bathroom stall, kissing me hard. The wall is cold on my back, but the heat of their body warms me through our clothes, making my insides tingle.

I kiss them back, playing with their tongue, biting their lip. I'm melting in their arms, sliding my fingers around the back of their neck. Their taste, body, lips, hands, the haze from the alcohol… all of it mingles in a dizzying rush of pleasure.

"You taste like a pastry," I say, aware as the words come out that I'm ridiculously drunk.

Lou lets out a breathy laugh that tickles my lips. "What kind of pastry?"

I kiss them again, then hold their face in my hands as I run my tongue over their lips.

They let out a soft moan, gripping my hair.

"Apple strudel, I think. Sweet, cinnamony—"

Lou claims my mouth before I can finish, moving their tongue in a way that leaves me weak-kneed. Our bodies arch together. I'm dying to get closer. I want to feel their weight on top of me.

"I don't want to—keep you from your friends," I say between kisses, some semblance of guilt winding through me.

"Shh. They're too drunk to notice I'm gone."

"Okay. Good." Maybe it's selfish but an excited swoop overtakes the guilt.

Lou traces a finger along my cleavage, and pulls my dress down. The material moves easily, and I suddenly like my outfit a lot more than I did a few minutes ago.

They tease my nipple and I gasp, the sensation crackling through me.

Lou gives me a wicked smile before dipping their head and flicking my nipple with their tongue. I bite my lip to stop from making a sound that would give us away. Though if anyone peeks at our shoes, there's no questioning what's going on in here.

I run my hands down their chest, stomach, and around their waist, relishing the feel of their toned body. They definitely work out. God, I want to see them naked.

I'm breathing hard, aching between my legs. I reach down and fumble with their belt.

Lou puts their hands on my shoulders and pulls back, stopping me gently, their expression pained. "Wait."

"Sorry," I whisper, my heart sinking. "I didn't——"

They kiss me quickly, silencing me.

"Claire, I like you," Lou whispers. "At the bar, I thought… You're really cute. And I think there could be something between us. Which is why I think we should stop here. Can I… um, can I take you on a proper date?"

I blink. *A date? With Lou?* "You want to go on a date with me?"

"Yeah. I know you just had a breakup and wanted a rebound, but… I'd like to be more than this." Lou motions to the decrepit bathroom stall. "I want to buy you dinner and drinks, and after a couple of dates we can, you know, see about picking up where we left off here. But maybe in a bed instead."

I smile. For the first time tonight, my sadness dissipates. I might be a mess, but I guess I'm still lovable. "I would like that. A lot."

Lou lets out a breath, casting a contagious smile. "Okay. Good."

We kiss again, and oh, I could do this for hours.

We exchange numbers, then take turns doing what we actually came into the bathroom for.

On the way back to the bar, Lou kisses my cheek. We're still tipsy, and now giggly as well.

"Ah, that'll be the girls," Lou says, pulling out their phone and looking at the screen. "One more stop for pizza, and then it's time for my favorite part of clubbing."

"Yeah? What's that?"

"Going home and—"

"Ooh, taking off your makeup and sliding into bed in blissful silence?" I say.

They laugh. "You know it."

"I think I'm going to do that right now." I catch sight of Michelle and touch Lou's back in farewell. "Text me?"

They nod, and damn, I'm a lucky girl. I came here a mess, reluctantly deciding to try and get laid to redeem some self-confidence—and I found something so much better. I found exactly who I needed.

I hope I was exactly the person Lou needed tonight.

Lou straightens their tie and puts their hands in their pockets, easily the most stunning person in this whole club. "See you on our date."

Forbidden Scripts

When best friends find themselves with a valuable heirloom, they flee from the dangerous people who want it—and in the height of adrenaline, their true feelings come out.

In the rearview mirror, two motorcycles barrel down the highway, weaving through traffic as they try to catch up.

I curse, accelerating until my SUV groans with the effort.

"Faster!" Suki yells from across the bench seat, her fingers digging into my upper arm.

"I can't steer if you're holding my arm!" I shout.

"Sorry!"

I want to hold her and protect her as I drive but I need both hands on the wheel and my full attention. I've never driven so fast in my life, and every sense is tingling.

Suki brings her knees to her chest and curls into a ball, her usual position when we're watching movies on the couch. And like a movie night, she's in sweatpants and a hoodie, her dark hair in a messy bun. I'm in full-on pajamas.

When she asked me to come over earlier, I thought we'd be chilling and eating chips.

"Fuck, I shouldn't have brought you into this," she says, making fists in her already messy hair. "Thea, I'm so sorry. This is all my—"

"No, it's good that you did," I say firmly. "You shouldn't face this alone. We'll figure this out, okay?"

I mean it. I'd do anything for this girl, and I think our current situation proves it.

I weave between the moving cars like they're sitting still, passing them recklessly. The steering wheel shudders. My hands throb from gripping it so tightly.

The road conditions are awful—rainy, slick, the sun plunging us into darkness as it sets behind the clouds. If a car cuts us off, if my tires lose traction, or if I clip a sign as we zoom by on the shoulder, I'm going to lose control.

But I don't want to think about what'll happen if those motorbikes catch us. When those men showed up outside Suki's door, that was the first time I'd seen a pistol in real life.

"Your grandma never mentioned the journal before she died?" I ask.

"No. I found it in her attic when we were cleaning out her house. I didn't think..."

The journal sits in Suki's lap, ancient, leather-bound, with a symbol that looks like an eye embossed in the center.

Why would Suki's grandma own something that men with guns would come after? What could they possibly want with it?

"She obviously had it for a long time," Suki says, craning her neck to look out the rear window. "It wasn't until I posted a picture of it on Instagram that the cryptic messages started coming in—strangers offering me money, threatening me, telling me to mail it somewhere because it's not mine to own."

"But what's *in it* that could possibly—"

"Thea, they're catching up!" Suki yells.

I curse, checking the rearview mirror. Damn, these motorbikes are fast.

"Hold on tight." I hit the brakes and crank the wheel, driving into the median.

Suki screams as we bump through the ditch and over the grass, and I'm grateful for seatbelts. The hairbrush and lip balm in my cup holder bounce out and hit the floor.

On the other side, traffic flows steadily in the opposite direction. We don't have time to wait for a gap. I lean on the horn and accelerate, merging into the carpool lane whether the traffic is ready for me or not.

People honk and swerve, and there's a *thump* as someone clips the back of the SUV, but I straighten out and keep going.

"Are you okay?" I ask, a tremor going through me as I glance over.

"Yes. Eyes on the road!" Suki looks out the back window again, breathing fast. "I think that did it. I don't see them."

My heart is in my throat. These guys won't give up that easily. It's a matter of time before they catch up again.

"Where's the nearest police station?" I ask. I drove us all the way out to a rural part of town, and I don't know this area well enough to figure out where to find help.

"Not until I figure out what the notebook means," Suki says. "I can't risk anyone asking me to hand it over. What if it's something she wanted me to have?"

I don't know how to respond. On the one hand, we're being chased by two men with guns because we have something they want, so this seems like a good time to go to a police station. On the other hand, I don't want to tell Suki what to do with a family heirloom, and I'm *really* curious about what the heck this journal contains.

She turns on an overhead light and opens the journal, studying the handwriting. The pages are full of vertical text. The weird thing is that the characters are totally illegible. Nobody in Suki's family could figure out what the pages say, and the internet was of no help. It's like the journal was written in a language of its own.

The way she's hunched over the book, her fingers tapping the edge, loose strands of hair touching the page, reminds me of all the time we spent studying after school. How many times did our study sessions stretch on for hours as we enjoyed each other's company? And how many of those hours did I spend secretly making heart-eyes at her, wishing we could be more than friends?

A lot. And I'm doing it again.

I force my attention back to the matter at hand. "Okay. We'll stay hidden and figure out what this book means before we get help."

I feel her gaze on the side of my face. She looks at me like this sometimes, a complicated thought process going on behind her brown eyes. I wish I knew what she was thinking. I know what I *want* her to be thinking, but I'm probably wrong.

After a moment, she says quietly, "I seriously owe you."

"You don't. Let me be your ride or die, Suki."

In my periphery, she gives a weak smile. It's something I said to her as a joke the day we met in tenth grade, when she was the new girl and I was assigned to show her around.

Ride or die. I bite my lip to hide a grimace. I never would've guessed that we would be in this position three years later.

I veer onto the shoulder to pass a few cars and exit the highway. Night falls as we barrel down a rural road, plunging us into blackness. I pass two and three cars at a time, praying for no oncoming traffic. Headlights illuminate the inside of the car in bursts. The windshield wipers scrape loudly, filling the silence.

"Your grandma was a great woman," I say, glancing at the mysterious book. "Remember when we—"

"The sleepover," Suki says, some tension leaving her shoulders.

I grin. "Still the best sleepover ever."

Around a curve, we pass a semi-truck going the opposite way, and my heart jumps as I struggle to keep my SUV centered in the lane while going double the speed limit.

"I can't believe my grandma let us watch a Stephen King movie that night," Suki says.

"It was fun, though."

"So fun."

She's probably remembering the movie for different reasons than me. If I'm honest with myself, that night was definitely my queer awakening, and I wouldn't have said no if she'd leaned in to kiss me.

Prom was coming, so we decided to watch *Carrie*. We ended up clutching each other under a blanket, and I'll never forget the butterflies inside me as I rested my head on Suki's shoulder and held her hand, pretending to be more scared than I actually was. I remember the feel of her warm body against mine, her soft skin and hair, the sweet smell of her.

Then, when it was time to sleep, her grandma only had one guest bed. We cuddled under the guise of being scared after the movie, but for me, it was more than that. I remember playfully kissing her nose, and she laughed and blushed. We fell asleep in each other's arms.

We never talked about it, and I never found out what her feelings were that night—whether she was cuddling because she wanted to touch or if she was just being a friend. Neither of us has ever dated anyone, and we've never talked about crushes.

"Remember we ate her entire tin of cookies?" Suki asks, pulling me from my thoughts.

I moan. "I still dream about her chocolate chip cookies. Tell me you have the recipe."

"I do. I promise I'll make ten batches if we—"

Behind us, in the distance, a semi-truck lays on its horn.

We both gasp.

Suki peers out the back window, looking like she might vomit.

If that horn was the semi-truck we passed moments ago, then there is a real possibility that the motorbikes are catching up, and they just nearly slammed into the semi while passing the cars behind us.

I accelerate, on the edge of losing control of my vehicle.

Rain beats hard on the roof. The windshield wipers scrape.

"Do you think they'll kill us?" Suki asks quietly.

"Fuck," I say, the word bursting from my lips. I take a hand off the wheel to reach over and lace our fingers together. "I won't let that happen, okay?"

Suki squeezes back, breathing deeply, like she's on the brink of breaking down.

I curse under my breath.

I want to make this situation better. Seeing her like this is making everything inside me spiral. It's hard to breathe. I could be about to lose everything that makes me happy.

"I have to tell you something," I say, the words spilling out. I've spent too long not knowing, and I don't want to die without saying it.

"What?" Her voice is high with emotion.

"If we… If something does happen to us…" My mouth is dry. It's hard to get the words past my lips. "I want you to know that I love you."

"I love you too, Thea. You know that."

"No—" I shake my head, putting both hands back on the wheel. My heart is ready to burst out of my chest. "I'm *in love* with you, Suki. Like, your smile is my favorite thing in the world, and I miss you whenever I'm not with you, and my heart feels like it's literally expanding every time I look at you."

Suki falls quiet.

Regret bubbles inside me. I shouldn't have admitted that. I don't know what I was thinking, and I don't know what I expect her to say. This isn't the right moment to confess my feelings.

"You don't have to say anything," I say, heat rising in my face. "I just wanted to tell—"

"I love you too," she says, her voice thick.

I glance at her, stunned. "You do?"

Her eyes are watery. She swipes a hand across her cheek and nods, smiling. "You're the best thing in my life, and the only person I want to be with."

I choke out a laugh, my insides doing backflips. "Then we sure as hell better get out of this alive, and remind me to kiss you when it's all over."

She laughs too, and the sound gives me the energy I need to keep driving.

I bite my lip, torn between smiling and crying. Why did it have to take this possible-death experience for me to admit my feelings? I should have told her months ago. Years ago.

I drive faster. For Suki, and for any future she and I might have, I need to get us away from these guys.

We're about to pass a service road leading into a forested area when Suki shrieks for me to turn down it.

"Go off-road. Turn off the car when we're in the bush. We've got the advantage of four-wheel drive."

I do it, wishing we were close to a busy supermarket instead. But hiding in the woods is better than driving aimlessly in an unfamiliar place.

We bump over the gravel road, my insides sloshing with every pothole. When I turn off the car and headlights, the world beyond the windows is pitch black, the forest blocking out the twilight.

The interior lights are still on. Suki and I look at each other across the bench seat, panting, terror hanging thick in the air between us.

She reaches up and turns the interior light off, plunging us into blackness.

I lean against the headrest, catching my breath. Sweat prickles under my shirt.

Absolute darkness and silence engulf us.

In the distance, the sound of motorcycles draws nearer.

"Fuck," Suki says, her voice cracking.

"It's okay. It'll be okay," I say, trying to convince myself just as much.

Her seatbelt clicks, and the leather groans as she slides closer. Her fingers close over mine, and she leans against me, her soft hair tickling my neck.

As I squeeze her hand, the motorcycles grow louder.

Louder.

We might have seconds left before they find us, and we're trapped in the woods, totally vulnerable. They could shoot us both, take the journal, and leave, and it would take days or weeks for anyone to find our bodies.

I angle my face toward Suki, my eyes closed, focusing on the feel of her breath against my face, her fingers entwined in mine, her head resting on my shoulder.

And then—

Zoom.

The motorcycles blow right by.

Their sound fades into the distance.

They're gone, and we're back in silence.

Suki slumps beside me.

The tension drains from my body, leaving me depleted.

We did it. We lost them.

"Thank God," I whisper, rubbing my face.

My heart pounds in my ears. Our breaths are quick and shallow. The outside world is all heavy rain.

"Do we drive back the way we came?" I whisper.

"Let's wait," Suki says. "Give them time to get far away."

"Okay." I stare ahead into the blackness, willing my heart to slow down.

I'm on the point of wondering what we'll do to pass the time when Suki's soft hand slides around the back of my neck, sending a pleasant shiver down my body.

"Now's as good a time as any," she whispers.

My breath catches.

I sense her moving toward me—a rush of warmth, her soft breath, the groan of the leather seat.

We kiss, and I part my lips, welcoming her eagerly.

This is everything I've been aching for. Her sweet scent fills me, and her taste is even better. I suck on her lower lip and tongue her gently, needing more. Her skin is soft and cool beneath my hands.

Our adrenaline makes us move faster until we're rocking feverishly against each other, our mouths locked, grabbing each other's clothes. She pulls me hard toward her.

I hold her close and kiss her with everything that's been building inside me all these years. Wayward strands of her hair tickle my face and neck, silky soft.

"Thea," she says, gasping.

The sound sparks something in me. I struggle with my seatbelt, unbuckling it in a frenzy. I tease her earlobe with my tongue, making her moan, and graze my teeth down the soft skin of her neck.

Needing to be closer, I straddle her lap, my knees on either side of her thighs.

We fumble with each other's shirts, pausing our kissing for long enough to toss them aside.

Her skin is hot beneath my palms, begging to be kissed and licked. I wrap a fist in her mussed-up hair, and run my tongue down her neck, moving lower.

She moans, tracing her fingers up and down my body. I arch my back, pressing my hips and breasts against her. Her skin feels amazing on mine, soft and warm.

Before I can claim her mouth again, she dips her head and kisses my breast, moving toward my nipple. I gasp as she licks and sucks. My fingers tighten in her hair.

A tremor passes through me. I want her badly.

I reach between her legs and massage her through her sweatpants. "Can I?" I whisper, breathing hard.

"As long as you let me do the same," she says, and I can feel her smile against my lips.

"Okay." I slide my hand into her sweatpants, and she gasps.

The feel of her on my fingers is dizzying. I bite my lip, an unbearable burning sensation igniting low inside me.

"Oh, fuck," she whispers, reaching into my pants to do the same to me.

The way I'm straddling her lap, my legs open, her fingers feel so good that it's hard not to cry out. I brace my hands on the headrest, rocking my hips with the rhythm of her hand.

We massage each other, our hands moving faster, our breaths sharp. In the blackness, the whole world is just the sound of her breaths and moans, the feel of her body against me, the taste of her lips and skin. Sweat prickles on my skin as the SUV warms.

"How come it took us so long to admit it?" Suki asks, panting.

My brain is slow, dizzy. "Afraid of—wrecking our friendship—maybe."

"I wouldn't call this wrecking anything. God, you feel good." Suki pushes me sideways and gets on top of me, pinning me down on the bench seat. She opens my thighs wider, making me moan.

I undulate my hips, losing control, heat building low inside me. I can't believe this is happening. I have to commit everything about this to memory, because after tonight, who knows what'll happen.

Suki trembles above me, crying out as I finger her and bite her neck. It's unbearably sexy to see her lose control like this. My body is responding, trembling, wet, and the noises coming out of my mouth are totally involuntary.

"Yes, yes!" Suki says, gasping. "Right there."

"Me too." I tilt my hips, my whole body tightening, until the heat inside me reaches a peak.

My body releases, and I lock my lips onto hers, stifling my cries. I'm disoriented, detached from the world completely as waves of pleasure ripple through me.

Suki climaxes with me, shuddering, gasping as if trying not to scream.

As we come down, she's panting hard, and kisses me twice with tired lips.

I link my fingers in hers, catching my breath, dizzy with ecstasy.

After a moment, she whispers, "When did you know you had feelings for me?"

I'm glad it's dark because I blush. "I think around the time of the infamous sleepover."

Suki hesitates. "I think that's when I knew, too."

"Seriously?"

"It was nice cuddling that night. I kept imagining kissing you and… more."

"Wow," I whisper. "Who would've known that a sleepover with *Carrie* and the tin full of cookies…" I trail off, something sliding into place in my memory.

"Mm," Suki says sleepily, resting her forehead against mine.

"Suki, your grandma's cookie tin had an eye symbol on it."

"What?" she asks, her tone sharp.

"Was it the same symbol as the one—"

"The journal! Holy shit." She lunges for her phone.

I sit up as she uses the flashlight to illuminate the journal on the floor, where the eye is embossed on the cover.

That's the one. It's the same symbol as on the tin.

In the glow, I can't help but trace my gaze over Suki's naked upper body. I don't think I've ever seen a more beautiful sight.

She catches my eye, and her face breaks into the most radiant smile in the world. "You're onto something."

"Really?"

"The cookie tin came from her sister in Japan—which means I think I know where this book came from."

I smile back. "Let's get our shirts on and get out of here. We've got plane tickets to book."

"Yeah?"

I nod. "Wherever you need to go, Suki, I'll be right there with you."

The String Bikini Castaway

When a paddleboarder tries to head out on the water on a windy day, she has to get rescued by a cutie in a canoe.

With my black string bikini hugging my curves, my blond hair in a high ponytail, and a golden tan, I carry my paddleboard down to the beach with purpose. I'm going to post such smoking hot pictures today that Tara is going to rue the day she dumped me.

Between this outfit, this smile, and this confidence, I am *flourishing* without her.

The June morning is crisp, raising goosebumps on my skin. A few other cars are in the parking lot but it's early enough that it's just kite surfers and kayakers. The lack of crowds should make for a peaceful time on the water.

At the shoreline, I turn on my GoPro, and strap the paddleboard's leash to my ankle. I toss my dry bag aboard next to my life jacket, which will have to hang out at my feet because it'll look dorky in pictures.

As I step into the tide, the wind whips strands of hair in my eyes and pulls my board every which way. The waves hit my thighs, and I gasp. Holy crap, it's cold.

Maybe the sight of all the kite surfers should've tipped me off that it's too windy to paddleboard. But I spent a long time doing my makeup and drove an hour to get here, so I need to get at least one good picture.

"Okay, let's get this over with," I mumble.

Not usually the way I start a day of paddling but the wind isn't exactly making this fun.

Last time I paddleboarded, Tara was with me, and the day was sunny, hot, and perfect. We had precarious sex on her board underneath the pier. It was bold and adventurous, and so typically *her*. It was the moment I realized she always made my day more fun, and the moment I knew I wanted to spend the rest of my life doing exciting things with her.

Then, a week later, she dumped me. Told me she didn't love me anymore.

Fuck her, anyway. I'm hot and lovable, and she's going to see me having sexy fun without her in these photos and regret her choices.

I kneel on the board, and after a struggle with the paddle, a gust pushes me away from the shore. I try to stand but a wave rocks the board, and I fall to my knees.

I grit my teeth. I can do this. I just need to stand for long enough to take a picture.

But after a few minutes of struggling, the wind is getting stronger—and when I look back at the beach, my heart leaps into my throat.

I've drifted a long way from where I started, and am way too far from the shore for comfort.

I grab the paddle and dig into the waves, aiming for the beach. The wind pushes me sideways, making it impossible to steer.

"Oh, shit," I whisper.

I grunt with the effort of paddling, using all my strength.

It's not enough. The swells are getting higher, and the wind is a harsh mistress.

I put on the life jacket, past caring how dorky it looks.

Great. I just wanted some hot pictures to make my ex mourn me, and now I'm about to become a castaway.

Mother Nature pushes me around a bend, where the beach turns into a forest.

I'm too far out to swim to safety, and I'm officially scared. I've paddleboarded for years, and I've always been able to get back to shore. What now? Will the waves push me to shore eventually, or am I going to drown out here? Maybe I should get my phone out of my dry bag and call someone for help.

This is Tara's fault. I wouldn't be here today if she hadn't been totally heartless and broken up with me.

"Hey, are you stuck?" a faint voice asks, and I snap my head around to search for the siren call.

By the forested shoreline, there's a twenty-something woman in a red canoe. She's in a life jacket and snapback hat, her pale skin streaked with sunscreen, looking much more practical and prepared than me with my idiotic string bikini and no emergency equipment. I didn't even remember to put on sunscreen this morning.

A border collie in a red life jacket sits in front of her, its ears perked in my direction.

They're both probably judging the hell out of me right now.

"Wait. Rosie?" the woman says.

What—oh, *God.* It's Elise! I went on three dates with her last winter before she ghosted me.

"I'm fine," I say, gripping my swaying board for dear life. No way am I accepting help from her. "Just resting before I paddle back."

"Liar. There's no way you can paddleboard in this wind. You're spinning like a top."

I can't argue. The waves push me around so I'm facing away from her, and then back the other way, twirling me like I'm debris from a shipwreck.

"I'm coming. Don't move," Elise says.

"Couldn't if I wanted to," I mumble, at nature's mercy.

She paddles closer. "This is Maggie. She's friendly. Toss me the leash?"

For a moment, I think she's talking about the border collie's leash, and then I notice her pointing to the strap around my ankle.

"Oh. Yeah." I undo the velcro and toss it to her.

She fastens it to the canoe so my board won't float away, then turns back to me. "Okay. Ready for you. Maggie, stay."

Ugh, I really don't want to be rescued by some woman who ghosted me a year and a half ago, but what else am I supposed to do? Drown out of stubbornness?

Elise uses the leash to pull me closer, then kneels in the middle of the canoe and holds out a hand. I take it. She's warm and dry, and after thinking I was going to die alone out here, I don't want to let go.

She keeps the canoe balanced while I climb in. The waves send us up, down, up, down, our watercrafts bumping into each other. Maggie whines as I add to the unsteadiness.

I'm shaking and exhausted, and with a groan, I land between Elise's legs. My ass is on the bottom, my legs hanging over the side, one hand gripping the edge and the other on her inner thigh.

I take my hand off her thigh. "Sorry."

"Rosie, you're freezing," she says, running her warm hands up and down my arms. "Are you okay?"

The motion is intimate, and paired with the way I'm positioned, it makes me blush furiously. I swing my legs over so I'm sitting in the bottom of the canoe facing her.

"Yeah, I'm fine. I haven't been out here for long."

Our faces are close, and the waves nearly make me fall into her lap again. She smells like sunscreen and citrus. Meeting her hazel eyes, I remember why I was so attracted to her—and why it hurt so much when she never texted me back. She's as beautiful as ever, and still definitely my type—nerdy, outdoorsy, a dog mom, confident and chill. Her dark blond hair pokes out of her hat in a cute, short ponytail.

Why do all of the amazing women in the world dump me? Is there something wrong with me?

Elise clears her throat and returns to her seat, and I pretend to be occupied with my life jacket.

"Do you need water? A snack? First Aid?" She motions to the clutter around me. There's a lot of stuff in the canoe—bags, a cooler, ropes, floatation devices.

"I'm good, thanks. But you have solid emergency preparedness."

Elise smiles. A tingle goes through me. Though the tingle might be because there's a dog sniffing the back of my neck.

"Hello, Maggie," I say, rubbing her ear. "I've heard good things about you."

There's a *thump thump* as the dog's tail hits the side of the canoe.

Elise blushes and rummages in her pile of stuff—maybe remembering how she told me about Maggie on our dates. Before she ghosted me.

I'll never forget the night we went to an indoor go-kart track. It was the best date I've ever been on. The way she looked as she passed me in the little kart, with a dorky helmet on and a playful grin on her lips, made me break down into giggles that didn't stop for the rest of the evening. Her charm turned me to putty in her arms at the end of the night. Before parting ways, we'd made out against my car for several minutes, and the intoxicating feel of her hands running up and down my body kept me up for nights afterward.

"Where'd you start?" she asks, snapping me back to reality. She ties a yellow rope to my board so we can tow it behind us—and of course she knows how to do an intricate sailor's knot.

"First beach," I say, tearing my gaze away from her fingers.

"*The pier?*"

"Yeah…"

"Holy shit. The wind blew you far."

"I know. My arms are dying."

She laughs. "Well, it's not a great day for paddling."

"Don't need to tell me that," I grumble.

There's an awkward pause. I look at Maggie, who stares back. There's a lot of intelligence behind her brown eyes.

Elise tosses me a bungee. "Here, use this to fasten your stuff to the board."

"Thanks." I take it, and strap down my paddle and dry bag. I furiously cram my GoPro into the bag, shame licking through me.

"The scenery is beautiful along here," Elise says, motioning to the forested shoreline. "I'm sorry you couldn't enjoy it today."

"It's fine. I wasn't really out here to—" I shut my mouth, heat rising in my face. Wow, I must sound like an idiot. So I wasn't out here to enjoy the scenery and experience, but instead to get bikini pictures?

Ew, who *am* I?

"I think karma got me," I say.

Elise raises an eyebrow, waiting for me to go on.

I push my board away so we can get going, avoiding her gaze. "Honestly, I was hoping to get cute photos so I can post them on Instagram and make my ex regret dumping me."

There's a pause, and then Elise lets out a laugh. "An admirable plan. Well, you do look super hot, if that makes you feel better."

"I—thank you—" A flutter swoops through my chest, which I ignore. Yeah, she was forward when we went on our three dates.

I check her out, hoping she can't see what my eyes are doing behind my sunglasses. She's as hot as ever, and I can't help but admire the way her arms flex as she dips her paddle in the water.

"What if your ex doesn't check your Instagram?" she asks.

"Who *doesn't* check their ex's social media?"

"I don't."

"Well, you're—an anomaly." Crap, am I weird for checking on my exes?

No. That's totally normal and lots of people do it. I even tried to creep on Elise way back when, but her profile is private.

"How long ago did you break up?" she asks.

"Two weeks." I grab the spare oar from the bottom of the canoe, and get in the front seat to help paddle. My back is to her, which is better than if we were in a rowboat and had to stare into each other's eyes the whole way back.

Maggie sits in the middle of the canoe and stares at the water intently, like she's been tasked with keeping an eye out for fish.

"You shouldn't have gone out paddling by yourself," Elise says.

I twist around in the seat to glare at her. "You're canoeing by yourself!"

She motions to the bags on the bottom of the canoe. "I've got a lot of safety equipment with me."

"I see that. You look like you're on a Scouts adventure."

"And you look like you're on a quest to be a brand ambassador. Hashtag bikini babe. Use the code ROSIE to get ten percent off."

I scowl but it only lasts a second before I break into laughter. "Touché."

"Anyway, you remember how I am."

"I sure do." I shouldn't be surprised that she's ultra prepared for a little canoe trip. For our second date, she sent me an itinerary for our dinner-movie night, along with a Google Maps link in case I got lost. Her hobby also caught my interest.

"Are you still doing search and rescue with Maggie?" I ask.

She hesitates. "No, actually."

"Oh?" I face forward and start paddling. The shoreline looks a lot nicer from the safety of a canoe—thick roots tangling along the earthy shoreline, mossy boulders that would be good places to stop for a picnic, glimpses of a hiking trail through the trees. *This* is why I like paddling.

"It was cool for a time, and I miss it..." Elise says, "but when things get real, you realize it's not all a fun adventure, and people's lives could be lost."

"Is that why you stopped doing it?"

Another pause. "We lost a team member when we were pulling a skier out of an avalanche. That kind of thing sticks with you for a while."

My heart squeezes. "Oh. Shit. I'm sorry, I shouldn't have asked—"

"It's okay. I've been to therapy, and I'm dealing with it."

I paddle some more, searching for the right words. How awful. I can't imagine what that would feel like.

But why is she telling me this? We went on a few dates and had our tongues in each other's mouths, but we're basically strangers.

"Um, I didn't text you back because that was when it happened," she says, a tremor in her voice. "The avalanche thing. I couldn't pull myself together enough to think about dating. I'm... sorry I left you hanging."

My heart skips a beat. I don't look back at her.

So she didn't ghost me because she got bored? It wasn't about me?

"Don't apologize," I say. "I'm so sorry that happened to you. It's good that you took time to process it and go to therapy. And I'm glad you're doing better."

She says nothing.

Was that the right thing for me to say? Should I comment on how much I liked the dates we went on?

"You've got a couple of new tattoos," she says, swiftly changing the topic.

My insides twist. I hope I didn't make her feel bad for not texting me. I had no idea what she was going through, and now I feel like an ass for assuming she was being rude. I just really liked her when we went out. She was fun and a total flirt.

I can't bring myself to say this, especially since she obviously wants to change the topic.

"Yeah," I say, glancing at one of the tattoos she's talking about—a flock of birds on my wrist. "I'm up to six."

"Wow. That's a lot."

"Not really."

"It's a lot compared to someone who doesn't have any. What's the spiral by your elbow?"

I grin. "Oh. I was drunk. My bestie and I got matching ones in Havana. It doesn't mean anything."

She chuckles. "Will you get it removed?"

I look at her over my shoulder. "No. I like it."

She raises an eyebrow.

"I don't regret any of my tattoos," I say. "Or anything, really."

"You don't regret anything ever?"

I shake my head. "Everything's a worthy experience. The tattoos are moments in my life. I don't regret the drunk one because it makes me think of that chapter of my existence, and how much fun my bestie and I had together. The memory is part of who I am, and so is the tattoo."

"That's a nice way of looking at it. But I have a hard time believing you never regret anything."

A salty spray hits me, and I wince. Elise grins.

"Nope," I say. "Can't think of a thing."

As we paddle over the rough swells, pulling my board behind us, I have to admit I'm grateful Elise found me. I never would have made it back and probably would've had to call my dad for help.

My mind spins around the idea of regret, and how Elise might be letting it too far into her life. "Do you regret getting into search and rescue?"

She doesn't answer right away. Her paddle dips into the water five times, ten times. Finally, she says, "No."

"Good." I get into the rhythm of paddling, enjoying the way it feels to move over the water instead of fighting it. "You should get back into it, Elise. It's important work, and I'm guessing you're good at it. Based on the way Maggie stares at me like she's peering into my soul, I'm guessing she's smart enough to be great at it, too."

"She's a genius. And thanks for the encouragement. You never know. I might go back to it someday."

I look back at Maggie, who gazes at the passing shore like she's genuinely interested in sightseeing. It's pretty cute.

"So you're done with search and rescue, and now you canoe by yourself on weekends," I say.

"Somehow, you just made my life sound pathetic."

"I did not! Canoeing is cool."

"And retiring from search and rescue at twenty-five because I got scared?"

"It's amazing you did it in the first place."

We paddle in silence. What does she think of me, heading out on the water on a whim, with no thought as to what would happen if I got in trouble? She's calculated and careful in everything she does, and I'm over here with tattoos I got when I was drunk.

"I dated someone recently who hated canoeing," Elise says. "It always made me sad. We broke up a few weeks ago, so now I get to do it as much as I want. I've been going every weekend ever since."

"Ah, so we're both here today to spite our exes."

Elise laughs. "I guess so."

Except I'm being spiteful by trying to take a hot bikini picture, while Elise is out here doing an activity she loves. Trying to look at this objectively, my plan might not be very productive. If I'm going to post a hot bikini picture, I should do it for myself, not my ex. At least Elise is enjoying herself.

We get to shore, and I climb out of the canoe a little shakily. I need a stiff drink tonight.

Maggie jumps out, and sniffs around the beach while Elise and I get my paddleboard out of the water.

"You good to get home?" Elise asks.

"Yeah, thanks. I drove."

I take off my life jacket, which is cold, wet, and sticky.

"Okay, let me know if…" Elise trails off.

"What?"

She opens and closes her mouth. "That's—a nice bikini. Wow. It—um—it works."

I grin. She's *adorable* when she's flustered. "Thanks."

At least someone appreciates how hot I look today.

The sun peeks out, and a beautiful strip of light stretches across the ocean.

Our gazes catch. My heart skips a beat. Her hazel eyes pull me in, and I fight the urge to step closer.

"Thank you for saving me," I say. "I owe you."

"Stop. You don't owe me a thing."

"Not dinner to say thanks? Say, Friday at seven?" My heart leaps into my throat as the words rush out. I'm fully aware I might get rejected by her for the second time. But I have to try. When things ended between us, it wasn't because she lost interest, so maybe something is still there. Maybe the two of us could have a second chance.

Elise opens her mouth in surprise, and then she laughs, her whole face brightening. "On second thought, you owe me big time. Dinner sounds great. Then maybe I could kick your ass at go-karting again."

"Whatever. I would've won if you didn't ram me into the wall, you big cheater."

My body feels light, like the wind could carry me into the sky. I can't believe I'm getting another chance with her. She's absolutely stunning, and the longer I look at her, the weaker my knees get.

"Hey, do you want me to take that picture you came here for?" she asks.

"Nah. I'm good."

She's not moving. It's as if she's not ready to leave— and neither am I.

I clear my throat, my cheeks burning. "Actually, um… We're both out here to spite our exes, right? Maybe we should, like, post something that would make them jealous."

Elise raises an eyebrow. A cute smile plays on her lips. "Like what?"

I grin. "I don't know. We could kiss."

She steps closer. "To make them jealous?"

I step in until we're nose-to-nose. "Right."

The wind whips our hair, and sends a ripple of goosebumps up my body. The sun illuminates her eyes, drawing me all the way in.

We close the distance, and she's as soft and strong as I remember. Her hand caresses my cheek, and I slide mine around to her lower back. I hold her against me, an explosion of fireworks going off inside my chest as we move our lips tenderly against each other.

I guess I don't need to take a picture today. The memory of this will stay with me without the help of a camera—just her, me, Maggie, and the wild waves lapping at our feet.

The Witch of Lake Erie

When Angee breaks the promise she made to a witch, tension brews between them.

So I *might* have pissed off a witch.

Hundreds of spiders are crawling on the walls of my bedroom, coming shortly after yesterday's incident where snakes fell out of my car when I opened the door.

Yeah, they could be weird coincidences, but let's not live in denial. It's a hex. A gentle one, like a warning. If Callisto really wanted to get revenge, she would.

Shuddering with the heebie-jeebies, I get the vacuum and start sucking up the spiders. Waking up on a

Monday is awful on the best of days but this is pure torture.

"I'm sorry, little spideys," I say with a tremor in my voice. "She gives me no choice."

If there was one spider or even a handful of them, I could trap them under a cup and dump them outside like usual. But there is no cup big enough to trap this patchwork quilt of arachnids.

My hands tremble as I work the vacuum. If one of them gets on me before I can suck it up, I may scream.

It's been five months since I went to Callisto with bloody scratches all over me and a black cat that was actually a chimera in disguise. She fixed it in an afternoon, healing my cursed wounds, transforming Toby back into a fire-breathing monster, and banishing him from this world.

I miss Toby but it's better this way. Ontario provincial laws prohibit keeping chimeras as pets, and I don't want that on my record.

The conditions of Callisto's work were straightforward: pay the invoice within three months, and don't adopt any more animals in case there's an ancient curse on me.

I honored the first condition and paid her in a few weeks. I have a good job as a dental hygienist, and was able to pay her in installments. But not adopting a replacement pet after I lost my darling Toby?

It's lonely living by yourself.

I thought I would be safe with two guinea pigs. There's no way these squeaky little bread loaves could be monsters in disguise.

And I don't think they are.

But I'm positive that Callisto found out I broke the terms of our agreement.

With an icy feeling in my chest, I recall the final step in her spell after she'd banished the chimera that was once Toby. She did something to me. It passed over me like a shiver. I bet she was placing a hex on me to ensure I'd be punished if I adopted another pet.

"Dammit." I cast a guilty glance at my guinea pigs, Rosencrantz and Guildenstern, who murmur happily in their cage.

I refuse to get rid of them. They were at the shelter for a whole year before I adopted them yesterday. They need me—and as a single introvert living in a big city, I need them.

But as I vacuum up the last spider, a rat scurries past my bedroom door, and a swarm of moths flaps through my window, which I swear wasn't open a minute ago.

All of the trapping and pest control in the world isn't going to fix this.

I call Callisto, and it goes to voicemail.

"You've reached Callisto O'Connor, Freelance Witch and Independent Apothecary serving Southern Ontario," she says in her deep, deadpan voice. It sends a pleasant tingle through me to hear it again. "Leave a message, and I'll get back to you as soon as possible. If this is an emergency that involves a hex, curse, or jinx, please hang up and text me instead."

I hang up and text her.

Hi Callisto, this is Angee Kumar. You helped me with my chimera problem a few months ago. I'm just wondering if you've hexed me, because I've got weird stuff happening in my apartment.

I call in sick to work, then devise a system to trap the rats without harming them while I wait for her reply.

An hour later, the rats seem to have multiplied, and my phone beeps.

You adopted a new pet, didn't you? Bring it to me today so I can inspect it, please.

I bite my lip to stop from smiling. I should be ashamed but the prospect of seeing her again sends a flutter of excitement through me. Despite all the panic of my last visit, it was one of the best days of my life. I'd never seen a witch work before, and watching her mutter spells and mix ingredients was incredible.

I type a reply.

I adopted two guinea pigs... I'm sorry. I'll be there in 3-4 hours. If they're not cursed, can I keep them?

Dots appear to show that she's typing, and then disappear. My heart beats faster. She *has* to say yes. Who hexes someone for rescuing animals from a shelter?

The dots appear again, and her reply comes through.

Yes. If they're safe, you can keep them and I'll reverse the hex I put on you.

I grin. Looks like I'm making a trip to the shores of Lake Erie today.

* * *

By nine a.m., I'm dressed, my hair is brushed, I've got light makeup on, and I'm ready to go. I'm in a ridiculously short ivory dress that looks like it was made out of doilies—my bridesmaid dress for my friend's wedding two years ago. The cursed moths got to everything else in my closet, and this was the only thing that survived because it was safely in a garment bag.

And it's way too cold to wear in early spring in Canada.

"You owe me a new wardrobe, Callisto," I mumble.

I load Rosencrantz and Guildenstern's cage into the trunk of my hatchback, where they'll hang out and feast on fruit and vegetables during the three-hour drive.

Callisto lives in a farming town called Merlin on the coast of Lake Erie, where the land is sprawling and the houses are quaint. Fog casts a chill over everything when

I arrive, obstructing the view of the lake and making me shiver before I even get out of the car. Her home is a white farmhouse with a rose garden in front and a dozen greenhouses in the back. When I visited her in the fall, she told me she uses the greenhouses to grow plants that can be used in potions. I think witches get tax write-offs for that sort of thing.

I put Rosencrantz and Guildenstern in my messenger bag, and make my way to the door. The silence is chilling, especially after being in the city. My Vans crunch loudly over the gravel driveway, and my guinea pigs squeak softly by my hip.

The door flies open before I knock, robbing me of the chance to compose myself.

My heart leaps at the sight of her. She's in a floor-length black robe and strange makeup with symbols painted below her eyes. A tiny vial dangles from a black cord around her neck. Her skin is as pale as I remember, her hair white, her eyes the lightest gray.

"Hi—Callisto—" I stammer, heat building in my face.

Fine, I admit it, I totally have a crush on her. She's gorgeous, fascinating, gifted, and it takes a genius to run a business the way she does. After my last visit, I couldn't stop daydreaming about moving out here with her and making a job change from dental hygienist to lesbian witch assistant.

Callisto's gaze traces over my tiny, lacy white dress in a way that makes me self-conscious. When I put it on, I didn't consider that she would be wearing the total opposite.

"Angee. Come in," she says, as deadpan as ever.

I step inside and she shuts the door behind me.

The house is cozy, and from where we're standing in the living room, the kitchen, bedroom, and bathroom are all within a few steps. It's just like I remember—hot, humid, with the soothing smell of flowers and greenery. A fountain trickles on the coffee table, which is a tree stump that might actually be growing out of the wooden floor. It feels like stepping into a rainforest. Tapestries with symbols line the walls, and a large bookshelf holds neatly arranged jars of ingredients.

I clear my throat. "How have you b—"

"Pigs." She holds out her hands.

"Um, right." I reach into my bag, and pass over my furry friends.

She sets them on the wooden dining table, where she's placed a bundle of parsley, and holds her hands above them while murmuring a few words.

"Does parsley enhance the spell?" I whisper, stepping closer.

She raises an eyebrow. Rosencrantz and Guildenstern trundle over to the parsley and start munching on it, purring with happiness.

"It's to keep the guinea pigs in place," she says, and I shut up.

She moves her hands and resumes murmuring. A gold aura swells around the piggies while they eat the parsley, oblivious to their situation.

"People who end up with a chimera in their house are usually cursed," Callisto says. "That sort of thing doesn't happen by accident. That's why I advised you against getting more pets. A chimera might not be the worst of it."

I hang my head in shame. "Sorry."

She moves her hands and murmurs for another minute, and the gold aura pulses softly, like lungs inhaling and exhaling.

"But," Callisto says, "since it was a shelter cat, maybe the original owner was the one with the curse, not you."

She drops her hands, and the aura disappears. The guinea pigs squeak and purr as they devour the parsley, which I'm sure is extra delicious since it was grown by a witch.

When Callisto meets my eye, the faintest of smiles pulls at her darkened lips. "The piggies are perfectly normal."

"So… I'm not cursed?" I say, my heart lifting. "I'm allowed to adopt pets?"

She picks up Rosencrantz and Guildenstern, and offers them to me. "It would seem so."

"Yes!" I say, taking them and hugging them. "Hear that, guys? You're coming home with mama."

They squeal happily.

Callisto turns away, and I'm positive she's hiding a smile. "I have to admit, your dedication to rescuing animals is… sweet."

Now it's my turn to hide a smile. I drop my chin, running my thumbs over the guinea pigs.

"Makes me wonder if I should get a cat," Callisto says. "Would make it less lonely around here."

A girlfriend would help fix the loneliness, I think, and then blush.

God, I'm glad she can't read minds.

"You should," I say. "There are so many black cats at the shelter that need adopting."

She nods, cuffing her sleeves. "Time to fix the hex I put on you."

"Oh, yeah." Right to business. That's fine. "The moths ate almost everything in my closet, and the rats are multiplying. I left my place in a bit of chaos."

Callisto's gaze flicks over my tiny white dress again. Something about the way she's looking at me puts a flutter in my belly, and I stand taller.

"I'm glad the moths didn't eat that dress," she says. "You'd better sit. Come to the couch."

What does that mean? Does she like the dress? Is she being sarcastic?

I put the piggies back on the table with the bundle of parsley, then sit on the green velvet loveseat. Callisto kneels in front of me, positioning herself at my shins. My knees brush against her breasts—and I hope she didn't hear the way my breath just hitched.

She holds out her hands, palms up, and I hesitate. Does she want me to hold them?

"Come on," she says, wiggling her fingers.

Okay, I guess I am supposed to hold her hands.

I place my palms against hers. She's warm and soft, and a lick of fire goes through me as we touch.

She locks my gaze, kneeling in front of me, and my insides are doing backflips.

"Your pulse is racing," she says softly. "Are you nervous?"

"Something like that."

Her lips quirk.

She draws a slow breath, holding my hands, and begins murmuring.

A sharp pain goes through my hands like a static shock.

"Ow!" I cry, trying to pull back.

"Reversing a hex isn't as simple," she says. "I'm sorry, but this might hurt."

"I don't want it to hurt! Is this why you made me sit down? Ow, Callisto—"

She keeps murmuring. The pain intensifies, traveling up my arms, into my chest, down into my legs, up into my head.

I gasp, trying to break free. "Callisto, stop. This is—"

"Almost done."

She mumbles faster, holding my hands tighter, and I lose feeling in my legs.

When she finally lets go, I gasp for breath, slumping forward.

"There," she says softly, "that'll get rid of the spiders, moths, rats, snakes, termites, and scorpions."

"Termites and scorpions?"

She grimaces.

After a pause, she puts her hands on my thighs, holding my gaze. "Are you okay? I'm sorry. I didn't want to tell you that it would hurt because you might not have wanted to do it."

"Well, you were right," I snap, a little angry with her for putting me through all of this. "I think I would've just chosen to live with snakes in my car."

Her mouth twists, and I catch a glimpse of what might be regret in her light gray eyes. "I only put that hex on you because I was worried that you would adopt another cursed pet and get yourself killed. I needed to guarantee that you would contact me if you went through with another adoption."

"Good plan," I mumble, still a little pissed off, but also touched that she was trying to protect me from something worse.

She's still kneeling in front of me, her hands on my thighs. This tiny dress makes the touch more intimate. Heat builds low inside me.

"Thanks," I say, putting my hands over hers before she can pull away.

"Of course." She looks at my hands, unmoving.

My pulse is racing from the counter-hex—and accelerating. What is Callisto thinking about, and why hasn't she stood up and asked me to leave? She was all business when I walked in.

She's such an extraordinary person, and painfully beautiful. I want to be part of her life in some way other than a business transaction.

Again, I indulge in the fantasy of living here with her, just the two of us in the quiet countryside. We would stroll around the property hand-in-hand, dine on our home-grown vegetables, watch storms over Lake Erie from our back porch... I could adopt as many pets as I want, even goats and donkeys. We could build a life together, and I could help her tend her crops—and if we were feeling mischievous, we could have sex in the greenhouses.

Would she be open to romance or is her life too complicated for that?

I guess there's one way to find out.

"Hey, um..." I rub my thumbs over the backs of her hands. It's a subtle movement, but perfectly clear.

She doesn't pull back. She meets my gaze with her strange, almost colorless eyes. Her cheeks are pink. Is she blushing?

"Are you..." Oh my, how do I word this? "Would you be interested in datin—"

"I can't," she says.

I swallow hard, taken aback by her abrupt answer. "Oh. Okay."

"I'm sorry, Angee. It's not you." She pulls her hands out from under mine but stays kneeling in front of me. "It's not safe for me to be close with anyone. The International Coven has a lot of layers. I have enemies. Rivals. It's why witches live alone."

I nod, my heart aching. "Do you wish you didn't have to be alone?"

She doesn't answer. The purring guinea pigs fill the silence.

"I'm sorry you can't have people in your life," I say softly. "You deserve to be happy and surrounded by loved ones."

Her eyebrows pull down, and her shoulders drop a little. She searches my face, something complex going on behind her pale eyes. "Thanks. I'm sorry I can't give you a different answer, Angee."

This makes my insides twist. Does that mean she would have said yes to going out with me? Or is she being polite by saying sorry?

"Well, I had to take a shot," I say with a shrug, pretending this conversation didn't crush my heart into pulp. "You're the most captivating person I've ever met."

She smiles, and for once, she lets me see it. It takes the breath out of my lungs.

"You feeling okay?" she asks.

I tilt my head. I'm drained in more ways than one. "Meh."

So Callisto and I could never be together. She lives behind a door that's firmly closed.

My heart hurts, which makes me angry because how can I be heartbroken over something that never was?

As I gather the guinea pigs and Callisto walks me to the door, the air between us feels different. Both of us are trying and failing to act casual.

"Thanks for driving all the way out here. I'm sorry again for the hex, and for hurting you, and... all of it."

I bend to pull my shoes on. "Don't apologize. I appreciate you trying to protect me from ancient curses and chimeras and stuff."

She gives me a little nod, and reaches around me to open the door.

I step out into the cold fog, and in our mutual awkwardness, I forgot to grab my messenger bag with the guinea pigs in it.

I turn around to say as much, and she's standing a lot closer than I expected.

We're nose-to-nose. Her breath grazes my lips.

"S-sorry," I whisper. "I forgot—"

She doesn't step back. We're so close that the slightest movement would bring our lips together.

Her eyes gleam, something blazing hot stirring behind them. The symbols painted beneath them seem to brighten. A breeze catches locks of her white hair, bringing them forward to tickle my cheeks.

My lips tingle. My insides are doing flips. Wearing this skimpy dress, I feel the heat of her body against my skin.

"Forgot—my—" I whisper. What was I going to say?

"Oh, curse it," Callisto says, and closes the distance between us.

She kisses me, and I respond automatically, parting my lips and bringing my hands up to her face. Her full lips move against mine, urgent, and I respond eagerly. She tastes sweet, like mint and berries.

Her hands run down my neck, shoulders, waist, and hips, tracing over me in a way that makes me shiver. I comb my fingers through her thick hair and arch into her, wanting to feel her against every part of me.

My head is cloudy. All of my senses sharpen. God, her body feels amazing. Her skin is soft beneath my palms. Her lips are plump and so kissable.

Her hand grazes my bare thigh, and I suck in a breath as she teases me along the hem of my dress.

I run my hand down her chest, grazing my palm over the swell of her breasts.

Her breath hitches, and her fingers tighten in my hair. She opens her lips wider, her tongue playing with mine.

And then she pulls away, leaving me gasping, aching for her. I hold her hands, not wanting her to stop kissing me.

"I—I can't," she says, breathing hard. "I just wanted to kiss you. Just once. I'm so sorry."

I touch my lips, wishing her kiss would stay with me forever. "Once," I whisper, wanting more. *Needing* it.

She picks up my messenger bag, and passes it to me gently. The guinea pigs hum inside it.

I accept it, and we both struggle to keep our cool, smoothing our mussed-up hair and straightening our dresses.

"I'm glad you did," I say, tripping over my words. My tongue and lips are on fire. "Even if it was just once."

Callisto casts that smile that takes my breath away. "Please keep being you, Angee. Kind, pure, sweet. Keep adopting all the animals."

I smile back, her words putting a flutter in my chest. "I will."

I back up a step, not wanting to take my eyes off her. She stands there in her black dress with a hand on the door, biting her lip.

"Can I come to you if I end up under some other hex or curse?" I ask, the words spilling out.

She nods. "My business is always open."

"Okay."

As I turn away and head to my car, I bite my lip to keep from smiling.

If I'm invited back under that condition, then I might have to scour the entire province for every curse I can find.

The Witch of Lake Erie: Another Curse

After scouring the province for cursed items, Angee returns to Callisto with a creepy doll and a secret motive.

I toss the creepy-ass doll into the trunk of my hatchback, refusing to put that thing anywhere near me on the three-hour drive to the shores of Lake Erie.

On the way there, I get rear-ended, the check engine light turns on, and iTunes and the radio both refuse to play anything but *My Humps* on a loop.

This sequence of events is my third clue that the doll is cursed.

Despite it all, my heart does excited flips the whole way to Callisto's place, and as I turn into her driveway, I have to take a deep breath to calm my nerves. What if she doesn't want to see me? What if she *does*? If today goes how I want it to, we're going to do a whole lot more than fix a cursed doll today. But my hopes are too high. I should be grateful I got as much as a kiss last time, especially since she told me she can't be involved with anyone.

Across the property, Lake Erie is smooth and dark beneath the blue May sky.

I don't know why she's not answering my calls or texts today but she'd better be home. It took me weeks to find something cursed enough to bring her, and after finding the doll this morning, I wasn't about to bring it home with me and spend the night with it. We are getting rid of this right now.

The white farmhouse is bright and cheery, the rose garden out front in full bloom. It hits me that the roses are probably charmed to stay in bloom all year.

Oh, to be a witch.

I get out of the car, and adjust my jeans and red crop top, checking my reflection in the window. I curled my hair and wore makeup, and damn, I look hot.

Drawing a steadying breath, I open the trunk. It's a little sticky because of the whole rear-ending thing, but I get it open after a struggle. The doll is sitting up, staring at me with glassy blue eyes, and I'm instantly filled with a sense of hopelessness. I break eye contact, trying to shake the feeling. That was my first clue that this thing is cursed. Nothing but a supernatural force could give me such an instant feeling of doom—well, that, and my boss's name showing up on my call display.

The second clue is how the doll looks. She's pale, blue-eyed, brown-haired, wearing a frilly blue dress with tulips on it and little wooden clogs. She's old and there are imperfections all over her face, but her expression is angelic. Sounds fine, right?

No.

The moment I look away, she becomes something else in the corner of my eye. It's like when you're in a dark room and you catch a glimpse of your reflection in a mirror, and there's a half a second when you think it's a ghost or a murderer. The first time it happened with the doll, when I found her at the flea market, I gasped and jumped back.

"You saw it, huh?" the old lady selling her asked me.

"Saw what?" I said in total denial. Because when I looked back at the doll, she was normal again.

But I knew what I saw, and it's happening again in Callisto's driveway. In my periphery, the doll's eyes are red, her mouth is open in a silent scream of rage, her dress is black and tattered, and her little feet with the wooden clogs have morphed into crow feet.

I shift my gaze to her again. Blue-eyed, tulips on her dress. And then to Callisto's house. A demon in my periphery.

With a shudder, I grab the doll by the feet, holding her determinedly away from my body so I can't see her.

Before I make it to the front door, it opens, and I stop in my tracks.

A beautiful, willowy blond woman is leaving Callisto's house wearing the world's tiniest shorts.

Fury rises inside me, hot and bubbling, as she walks toward me with a pink tinge in her cheeks and a familiar giddy smile that I know all too well.

She's too busy biting her lip to notice me until we're strides apart on the gravel driveway.

"Oh!" she says, putting a hand on her heart. "Didn't see you."

She looks at the doll dangling upside down from my hand, and her perfect, plump lips pull into a frown. I can see the effect the doll has on her, like clouds blocking the sun.

"Who are you?" I blurt.

She opens her mouth as if startled by the question. Then she must notice the doll in her periphery because she lets out a little scream and jumps back with her hands over her mouth.

"Angee?" Callisto says from the front door.

My heart leaps at the sound of my name on her lips.

I look past the infuriatingly gorgeous blonde and find Callisto in the open front door, a hand on the frame, watching us.

She's in a black gown with a lacy bodice that leaves her pale shoulders bare. The skirt ripples out like a ball gown, the phases of the moon woven into the material with faint silver threads.

Like the other times I've seen her, her makeup is dark and symbols are painted below her eyes. Her white hair is in a thick fishtail braid over her shoulder.

"Um, hi," I stammer. "I tried to call—I brought—um, this is cursed." I lift the doll higher to show her.

"Okay. Come in."

I walk past the blonde and into Callisto's house. The familiar, earthy smell of the home meets my nose, warming me from the inside.

When the door shuts, I say, "Who was that?"

Callisto's darkened lips curve upward. "Why does it matter?"

"It—doesn't," I say with a scoff.

There's a pause. Her light gray eyes search me. Heat blooms in my cheeks.

"She was trying to sell me on her pyramid scheme potion ingredients," Callisto says.

"Oh."

She takes the doll from me, and a silence passes while we hold each other's gaze.

"Angee," she says, and I'm surprised to hear a tremor in her voice. "I—I told you I don't have room for relationships in my life. I meant it."

"Right."

The words sting a little, because although she's referring to my reaction to that woman, she also means she doesn't have time for me in her life.

Callisto frowns at the doll. "Where the hell did you find this and why do you have it? Don't tell me this was in a cage at the animal shelter."

"I bought it at a flea market."

"Seriously?" Her eyes widen. Something changes in the room, like an energy that makes my pulse quicken. "You shouldn't have touched this. What were you thinking? This is really dangerous."

"It is?"

"You're lucky you didn't get into a car accident on the way over."

"Actually, I d—gah!"

The doll moves in her hand. She contorts, bending backward, and her angelic face melts and stretches like hot wax.

Callisto swears. "It's feeding off the room. Quick, get me a cup of water from the sink."

"Water?"

"Hurry!"

The panic in her voice makes me run.

While she flings the doll onto the dining table and dashes to the shelves, I tug open kitchen drawers until I find a metal measuring cup. I fill it with tap water and walk carefully back to her.

"In the pot," she says, motioning to a cute rose-gold cooking pot on the table beside the doll. She scoops ingredients out of jars, and mashes them feverishly in a mortar and pestle.

I dump the water into the pot, where it immediately starts boiling.

This isn't the greeting I had in mind. It's not that I was expecting her to throw herself at me and kiss me, but I was hoping we could take a second to acknowledge the unresolved tension from last time.

Instead, she pushes me out of the way and dumps a mix of ingredients into the pot. She murmurs a few words, casting nervous glances at the doll on the table.

The doll is still contorting, her heels by the back of her head, her face stretched so long it's unrecognizable.

"I've been trying to call you today," I say.

"I thought you were just trying to... Can you bring me the obsidian on the windowsill?"

"The what?"

"The black stone!"

I rush over and grab it, and she murmurs something into it before tossing it into the pot.

"You thought I was trying to what?" I ask. I know this is a bad time but it's been months since I saw her, and I've thought about her every day.

143

"I thought this would be another incident like last month," she says, "when you texted me trying to convince me you had a cursed pasta machine."

"It was cursed!"

"You were using a bad recipe."

"I found it on Pinterest!"

She gives me a withering look.

Before I can defend the recipe, she closes her eyes and says something unintelligible.

A breeze sweeps through the house, moving the plants, curtains, and loose pages on the bookshelves. A chill passes over me. The ingredients in the pot bubble and spit, turning crimson.

Callisto's eyes are closed, so she doesn't see the doll roll over.

She doesn't see it stand up, its face warped beyond recognition, and walk forward.

I sway, dizzy with panic, all of the blood seeming to drain from my body.

The doll grabs the edge of the pot with its creepy little hands.

Finding my voice, I choke out, "Callisto!"

Callisto opens her eyes but it's already happening. The doll is going to dump the pot of boiling potion onto her.

There's no time to think about what to do. I lunge forward and seize the edge of the boiling pot. Before the doll can tip it onto Callisto, I shove it the other way hard, sending the bubbling contents all over the doll and table.

A piercing scream comes from the doll, filling the house, as it melts beneath the crimson potion. It warps and shrinks until it's a lump of plastic, material, and tiny clogs.

My hands are searing. I gasp, shaking out the pain. "I'm s-sorry. It was about to—"

Callisto grabs me and pulls me back a step, looking wide-eyed at the half-melted, sizzling remains of the doll. "I—shit—you did the right thing, Angee."

"I did?"

"I thought I had a few more seconds. Fuck. I was distracted."

The potion sizzles on the table and drips onto the floor, darkening and hardening like cooling lava.

Guilt washes over me. This is all my fault. First, bringing the doll here, and second, distracting her while she was trying to undo its curse. Now her table is ruined, and her house smells like rotten eggs.

What would've happened if I hadn't tipped the potion onto the doll? Would Callisto be the one in a melted, sizzling heap right now?

She motions for me to step further away from the table with her, running a hand over her brow. "Give it a minute to stabilize. Sometimes, curses so strong have an aftershock."

"I-I'm so sorry," I stammer, horrified with myself for hunting that doll down and bringing it to her.

Callisto glares at me, a dangerous flash in her light gray eyes. "You'd better be. How long did you spend searching for a cursed item to bring me?" Her tone is sharper than I've ever heard.

Well, she saw right through me. I shouldn't be surprised. It's obvious I didn't buy the doll because I thought it was cute.

"Um. I've been searching since last time. Please don't be mad—"

She puts her hands on my shoulders, holding me at arm's length. "Angee, what the hell? You're putting your life at risk for an excuse to come see me?"

"I like you! A lot!" I shout, past caring about being subtle about my feelings. "You're gorgeous and smart and incredible. I've thought about you every day since the first time we met, and I don't care if it's dangerous being involved with a witch, because there's nothing I want more in the entire world than to be with you."

Her breath catches. She lets go of me and steps back, breathing hard. She won't meet my eyes.

My heart is pounding. My feelings fill the room, and I need to know what she's thinking. Did I scare her? Or is that something else passing over her expression?

"Callisto, look at me," I say softly, stepping closer.

She won't do it.

"I'm sorry," I say, really meaning it. "I didn't realize the doll would be so dangerous. You're so calm and good at what you do. I guess I thought that fixing curses was easy for you, and it wouldn't be a big deal."

She shakes her head, scowling. "Angee, that was so..."

"I know." I step closer until we're inches apart.

She doesn't step away.

Finally, she meets my eyes.

There's a long silence. We're both struggling to catch our breath.

For the briefest moment, I swear her gaze flicks to my lips.

Is she thinking about the kiss? Because I haven't stopped thinking about it. I lay awake remembering the feel of her lips against mine, the sweet taste and smell of her, her soft skin beneath my palms.

Should I tell her, or will she not want to hear it?

My ears tingle, picking up on something before the sense of danger reaches my brain. In slow motion, Callisto's eyes widen, and she turns her head toward the half-melted doll on the table—and it hits me what I'm hearing.

Sizzling.

A light flashes.

With a whoosh, the melted doll bursts into flame, and Callisto throws herself at me before I can react.

I stumble back, and hit the shelves on the opposite wall, the impact reverberating through the tiny house. The wooden shelves dig into my back, painful enough to make me gasp, and all of the items wobble. Jars topple and shatter on the floor. Books fall over with thuds.

All the while, Callisto's body is over mine, a shield between me and the fire.

The flames roar, the heat stinging my face, forcing me to close my eyes. I scrunch my face against the explosion, gasping for air.

I lean into Callisto, my eyes shut tight, my cheek pressed into the crook of her neck.

A series of pops fills the house, and we both flinch. Something must hit Callisto because she jerks and lets out a yelp.

We sink lower, curling into each other, with me safely between her and the bookshelf—but oh, God, what happened to make her cry out? Did she get hit with something cursed? What if a sharp object pierced her?

Finally, the explosion dies down, and our panicked breaths fill the room.

There's smoke everywhere. I can hardly see.

I try to ask Callisto if she's okay, but no words come out. My throat is tight.

Heart slamming into my ribs, I run my hands over her back, praying I won't find an injury.

Her dress isn't torn. There's no wetness indicating blood.

"Thank God," I whisper. "You weren't hurt?"

"I think it was this tiny wooden clog that hit me." She picks up the doll's shoe on the floor beside us. At her touch, it crumbles into ash.

I swallow hard. "You could have been hit by something deadly."

"But I wasn't."

I run my hands over her again to be sure. Her head, neck, shoulders, arms, waist, hips, and back are intact. No blood, nothing protruding.

At the feel of her body beneath my palms, a totally inappropriate flutter passes through me.

We stay on our knees for a long moment, pressed against the bookshelf, broken glass around us, herbs and powder all over the floor. I'm wrapped safely in Callisto's arms, not a scratch on me.

Her breath tickles my lips as she looks at me.

"Please never endanger your life just to see me again," she whispers.

I nod, and we're so close that a lock of her white hair catches on my lips.

She brushes it away, then rests her hand on my neck.

I don't move. My breaths are shallow as I sit in her arms, not wanting her to let me go.

She moves her face closer, and then hesitates, like she's debating whether to pull back.

"Whatever choice you make is fine with me, Callisto," I whisper. "I want you to be happy."

It hurts, but as much as I want to be with her, I have to respect her decision if she doesn't want me in her life.

"That's the problem," she murmurs. "What makes me happy and what I'm supposed to do are two very different things."

I don't know what to say so I wait, savoring every second that I'm in her arms.

"This would be easier if you weren't so amazing," she says, barely audible. "So beautiful. So kind."

Something is erupting inside me.

Just when I think we can't possibly be any closer, Callisto leans in. She kisses me so gently that my lips tingle. A pleasant sensation rushes down my core, making me shiver.

Slowly, as if trying not to scare her away, I lift a hand to her cheek. She's as soft as I remember, and her taste is just as sweet. I think of strawberries, honey, and all of the herbs she grows.

I part my lips, inviting her in, and she kisses me deeper.

A flutter goes through me. We kiss harder, our tongues and lips moving hungrily. She grips my shoulder and holds me close.

I run my hands down her lacy black dress, feeling her curves beneath my palms, caressing her breasts, waist, and cautiously moving lower.

When I reach her hips, she moans, making a fist in my hair.

"Come to my bedroom before I change my mind," she says, breathless.

It is possibly the best sentence I've ever heard her speak—which is saying something because in the two times I've met her she's said things like "this will heal the cursed scratches all over you and stop you from bleeding to death."

She takes my hand and pulls me to her bedroom, and I trail behind her like I'm walking in a dream.

Her bedroom is like the rest of the house—earthy, warm, with a lot of plants and strange shapes on the walls. The bedding is plush, and a deep, mossy green.

As my gaze returns to Callisto, she's playing with her sexy black dress like she's considering taking it off. Is that a flush in her cheeks? Is she shy?

If she's never let romance into her life, maybe she's never done this before.

I start with my own clothes, peeling off my jeans and taking off my shirt. By the time I'm out of my bra and underwear, she's gazing at me with a fiery gleam in her eyes, her chest rising and falling as her breath quickens.

"Let me," I whisper, taking her hand and pulling her close.

She places her hands on my waist with a soft moan. I spin her around and unlace her gown, enjoying the slow unveiling of her body.

The moment she's in front of me in nothing but a lacy black bra and underwear, a primal urge overtakes me, pushing all other thoughts from my mind. I close the distance between us and kiss her fiercely, and she responds with the same eagerness. She's strong and firm in my arms, and I can't stop running my hands over every part of her, reveling in her body.

I remove her bra and underwear before pushing her down on the soft bed so I can get on top of her.

Callisto wraps her legs around me, and pulls my mouth to hers.

I rock against her, the friction between our bodies making me dizzy. I'm on fire, my insides burning, every part of me tight and trembling. Her hands glide down my chest and to my nipples, which she flicks and teases with nimble fingers.

I gasp into her mouth, tightening my grip on the duvet beneath her. I'm so ready for her that I can barely take another second.

She rolls me over, surprising me, and casts me a wicked grin. "I've thought of getting naked with you every night for weeks."

A thrill pulses through me at these words. "That makes two of us."

We kiss urgently, our hands roaming over each other's bodies, rolling across the bed as each of us tries to top the other.

Before she can get on top again, I pin her wrists hard and whisper, "Stay there."

"But—"

"Shh." I kiss her neck, chest, and circle my tongue over her breasts. I suck each nipple, making her gasp. She writhes beneath me, breathing hard.

I kiss her stomach.

I flick my tongue over her belly button. "You taste amazing."

Salty, sweet, making me want to devour her.

"Mm," she says, knotting her fists in my hair.

I run my tongue along her stomach and hip bones.

She's breathing fast, making little whimpering sounds that drive me wild.

I wrap my arms around her thighs, savoring the feel of her soft, smooth skin.

When I part her with my fingers and lick her, she cries out, sinking deeper into the bed. "Angee——"

I lick her softly, my eyes closed, getting lost in her. She moans and gasps, and I respond to what she likes. I change up the rhythm and push her thighs wider, and soon, she's trembling beneath me.

"Oh, fuck," she whispers.

I open my eyes to find her flushed, her eyes closed, her mouth open in an expression of total ecstasy. Her chest is heaving and she's gripping the duvet with white knuckles.

I slow my pace, teasing her with gentle kisses and pauses.

"Angee, please," she moans, begging me to keep going. She combs her fingers through my hair, making me shiver.

Oh, I like the sound of her begging.

I reach down and touch myself, needing it.

I want to keep her like this for a while. I don't want this day to end. What if this is the only day I get with her? What if, like the kiss last time, she tells me that this is the end of whatever we have?

But the kiss last time *wasn't* the end of it. She said it was but here we are.

It's like she said: what she wants and what she's supposed to do are two different things.

Witches aren't supposed to have partners, but what does that matter? She lives alone out here. Nobody needs to know that I stop in once in a while to go down on her.

I grin.

She's breathing hard, whimpering, her fist tightening in my hair.

I move my tongue faster, pushing her legs apart so I can taste more of her.

"Yes," she says, breathless.

I bring her to the brink, and she moans louder, gripping the duvet like she's about to lose control.

Her body tenses, and a shudder rolls through her. A warm breeze sweeps through the window and around the room, like the house is responding. It sends a pleasant tingle over me. The green curtains over the window flutter. A tapestry on the wall sways.

Callisto covers her face as she climaxes, like she's hiding her pleasure from me—from the world.

I keep licking her until the waves subside. She gasps for air, going limp.

"I enjoyed every second of that," I murmur, raising myself onto my hands and knees.

"You awful tease," she says.

As I lay beside her, she gazes at me with a soft, sleepy look in her eyes. I've never seen her with an expression so open and vulnerable, and it sends warmth trickling through me.

I run my hand down her body, needing to keep touching her.

She bites her lip, a smile in her light gray eyes. Her hand wanders low, and she rubs me gently. "Your turn."

I put a hand on her wrist, stopping her even though it's painful to do so. "First, answer something for me."

She furrows her brow, a flash of concern in her eyes.

"Is this a one-time thing or can I come back?" I whisper.

I want to know before we keep going. I don't know if it will make a difference for what we do but it'll make a difference in how I feel about it.

Callisto opens her mouth. There's a pause in which the whole world seems to stop spinning. I'm praying, wishing, begging the universe to give me the answer I want.

Finally, a little smile tugs at her lips, and her cheeks dimple. "I want you to come back," she whispers.

Another warm breeze sweeps through the room, and victory blooms inside my chest as she leans in for another kiss.

Bonus: The Side Effects of Dating a Witch

Angee and Callisto are still in bed for the first time, and now it's Angee's turn.

"Promise me you won't tell a soul about us, okay?" Callisto whispers. "You don't know who's connected to other witches, and if one of them finds out…" Her eyes widen as if she's just considered something.

Scared she's going to change her mind, I say quickly, "I won't tell. I promise."

We hold each other's gaze, and her breath tickles my cheeks. Something is shifting in her expression but I can't decipher it. I want to know more about what exactly will happen if other witches find out about us but I don't want to ruin this moment by asking.

So I stay silent.

God, she's the most beautiful person I've ever seen. I could spend hours lost in those light gray eyes.

"Are you sure you're okay with that type of relationship?" she asks.

"I'll do whatever I have to if it means I get to be with you."

Her eyebrows pull down, and she melts into me.

Her lips tease mine before she finally kisses me. It's slow, deep, her tongue playing with mine and tracing over my lips. I try to nip her lower lip in return but she's taken control, pulling back so I'm left wanting.

With a wicked grin, she wraps a hand in my hair to hold me to the pillow, and dips her head to kiss my throat.

Oh, I'm in trouble.

While tracing her other hand down my waist, touching me so gently that I shiver, she rakes her teeth along the sensitive skin of my throat.

I close my eyes, savoring the feel of her. She holds me in place, pushing my knees firmly apart so she can slide her palm between my legs.

"I hope you're ready to be here for a while, because I have a lot of pent up energy," she murmurs. "Side effects of a life of solitude."

I can only moan. I'm dizzy as she glides her fingers up and down. She moves so slowly that she leaves me aching, biting my lip, needing more. I can feel how swollen and ready I am. Then she speeds up, moving her fingers faster.

"Yes," I whisper.

She stops.

"Why…" I try to lift my head but she's still gripping my hair, holding me still.

She plants a hard kiss on my lips, opening my mouth with her tongue.

Then she kisses my chest, tracing her tongue down the center, down my stomach, and pausing to kiss my belly button. She holds my hips between her arms, her hands cupping my waist, as she kisses and licks me all over.

"I-I can't believe you're teasing me like this," I say. "First you make me wait all this time to kiss you, and now—oh!"

I gasp, gripping the duvet for dear life, as she grants me a long, slow lick.

"Oh, God, you feel good," I moan, closing my eyes.

She makes slow circles with her tongue, and the feeling shoots through me like fire. It's burning inside me, the flames traveling down my arms and legs, making it hard to breathe.

She grazes her palms over my inner thighs and the backs of my legs, up and down, up and down. The sensation of her cool tongue and her warm palms moving over such a sensitive part of me is too much to bear. I'm panting, my legs writhing.

She circles her tongue faster. Pauses. Flicks once, twice, then closes her whole mouth over me.

"This is how I die," I moan. "I thought you said you'd never done this before."

"I haven't," she murmurs. "But that doesn't mean I don't watch videos."

I grin. "That's pretty hot—oh, God."

She kisses between my legs, then gives me another long, slow lick.

The changes of rhythm keep me hypersensitive. I can't take it anymore. I'm burning, my insides so tight that I'm going to erupt.

"Callisto…"

Her name is all I can manage. My face is hot. Sweat prickles all over. I'm breathing fast.

She closes her mouth over me and moves her tongue faster.

I grip the duvet tighter. "Oh, God, I'm—"

Her palms trace up my stomach, so gentle, and when she flicks her fingers over my nipples, it's too much. I tip over the edge.

I cry out as waves of pleasure take control of my body, leaving me at Callisto's mercy. She keeps licking and sucking until I reach down with fumbling hands to hold her still.

When she raises herself to come lie next to me, she's wearing a smug grin.

And she earned it. Holy shit.

"That was absolutely incredible," I say, totally spent.

"Mm, I could tell you were enjoying yourself."

I nuzzle into her, wanting to stay like this for hours. There's nowhere I'd rather be than this warm, soothing home, which smells like earth and herbs and Callisto.

But if we're going to keep our relationship a secret, how often am I allowed to be here? Can I stay the night? Do we have to pretend I'm a repeat client?

Abruptly, Callisto sits up. She's perfectly still, like a deer in the woods.

"What—" I begin but she puts a hand on my thigh to silence me.

There's a knock at the door.

Something in the Chocolate

Emma is a reluctant volunteer at her work's Easter picnic, but when the colleague she has a crush on shows up, the day turns out to be not so bad.

"Step right twice, and then left twice, okay?" I shout.

A swarm of forty kids shriek before me, barely paying attention. I look skyward, wondering how I got myself into this. In the open field around me, my coworkers mingle and eat the chocolate eggs the kids scavenged for minutes ago. Overhead, the bright sun is warmer than the forecast said, leaving me prickly beneath my cable knit sweater.

I cock my hands in front of me like a bunny, hating my life. "Then you jump forward, and back, and hop, hop, hop. Got it?"

The kids keep yelling, jumping like popcorn in a frying pan as sugar courses through their systems.

I look around desperately. Where is Jory? She's the reason I came to the company picnic, and the reason I joined the office fun committee in the first place—which was, in hindsight, not my best idea. Surely I could come up with other excuses to spend time with her, but here I am, teaching my coworkers' kids how to do the bunny hop on a Saturday afternoon, all because she cast that devastating smile and said, "Hey, Emma, you should join the fun committee with me!"

I press play on the music, eager to get this over with. The bunny hop starts, the bubbly tune attacking my eardrums.

Trish from HR looks my way so I plaster on a smile. "Ready, kids?"

I'm so done. I'm quitting the fun committee tomorrow. It served its purpose: Jory and I are talking. It's time to ask her out and stop getting myself into these things. I don't like my job enough to volunteer at weekend socials.

When the song ends and the volume of the kids' screams reaches a peak, I beeline toward the white tent reserved for the fun committee and catering staff. We've stowed our bags there along with the presents we're supposed to hand out to the kids later. It'll be a good place to hide—and maybe find some sunscreen before my sun-deprived face gets burned.

Before I can step into the tent, the flaps open, and a five-and-a-half-foot white bunny wearing a blue vest steps out.

I scream.

Then I cover my mouth, embarrassed. "Sorry," I say through my hands. "You scared the shi—crap out of me."

I look around for children. We're alone.

The bunny waves at me. He doesn't speak, like any good theme park character.

"My dad let me watch *Donnie Darko* when I was eight," I say, needing to explain my over-the-top reaction. "Totally messed me up."

I'm not sure where to look. The giant glassy eyes? Is the person's face in the rabbit's open mouth? I think I see mesh. "Anyway, um, the kids are over there. I'm sure they'll be happy to see the guest of honor."

As the creepy bunny moves on and I scan the field for signs of Jory, my insides are doing flips. The prospect of asking her out makes me nauseous. What if I've been misreading what I thought was flirting? Plus, being coworkers complicates this. I don't want to look like I'm hitting on the new girl, and I'm sure Jory doesn't want to look like she's flirting with her coworkers at her new job.

Trish spots me and flags me down. "Can you help the Easter bunny hand out presents to the kids?" she asks in a bubbly, kid-friendly voice.

"Sure," I say, regretting not crawling into a hole when I had the chance.

I need to stop doubting myself. What Jory and I are doing *has* to be flirting. We chat on Slack all day every day, and none of it is work-related. It's about her love of hiking in the sun, and my love of rainy days and reading. It's about her litter of foster kittens named after flowers, and my betta fish named Carl. It's about her excitement over whatever meetup group she's joining that weekend, and my predictable plans to spend it reading and illustrating. I even opened up to her about my dreams of quitting this job and becoming a full-time artist, and she opened up about how she used to love drawing as a kid before her dad died and she lost her creative spark.

I can't be imagining the connection we have. We're open with each other in ways I've never been with anyone else.

While the bunny and I hand out cheap gifts and more chocolate to the horde of children, my energy drains. There are so many things I could be doing this afternoon. Like finishing my book.

"This event would be better if people could bring their dogs," I mumble to the bunny, who gives me two thumbs up.

We finally finish, and the bunny claps me on the back and raises the roof.

My insides seem to be sinking into the grass, which is mud now that all the kids have been tapdancing on it all afternoon. There's half an hour left before we have to start cleaning up. I guess Jory isn't coming.

There are a few extra chocolate rabbits at the bottom of the bag—presumably for the people who wisely didn't come today. I open a box and snap the head off while the Easter bunny beside me watches.

"Adults deserve your chocolate too," I say before he can judge me. "I'm here out of the goodness of my heart. And I'm regretting every second of it."

I take a giant bite, and let out a slow breath. The hit of milk chocolate makes me feel marginally better.

As the bunny and I walk back to the white tent, I say, "Sorry I'm being a downer. I thought the person I have a crush on was going to be here today. You're doing a great job. What entertainment company did we end up going with?"

We enter the tent, and the bunny reaches up to its big white head.

And beneath it—oh, fuck.

"Surprise!" Jory says. "The entertainer canceled last-minute, so I ran out to rent a costume."

My heart flips so hard that it knocks me off-balance. The blood drains from my face. "Oh, hey, Jory!" I say with numb lips.

Jory makes a jazz hand with the one not holding the bunny head. Her hair is in a messy topknot, her light brown skin has a sheen of sweat from the stifling costume, and her eye makeup is running a little—and she still manages to look stunning.

I'm dying. Did I say anything humiliating while we were handing out presents? Oh, God, I just told her—

"Who do you have a crush on?" Jory asks, a gleam in her brown eyes.

"No one. I was kidding. It's fine."

Come on. Like you don't know I'm totally in love with you.

She steps closer. The chemical scent of the costume mingles with her subtle perfume, confusing my senses. "Is it Trevor? Rae called him the only fuckable guy at the company."

Trevor? Does she seriously not know?

All this time I thought we were flirting, and she still thinks I'm into guys.

Or is she fishing for me to tell her I'm gay?

I open my mouth to tell her that I'm not into men but what comes out instead is, "Did Rae really say *fuckable*?"

"Not at the office," Jory says, a look of horror crossing her face. "It was when our team went out for drinks."

"Oh. Cool." I suddenly wish I was on their team instead of the support team. Going for group drinks would be an excellent way to start hanging out after work. We could chat, and then I could ask if she wants to keep hanging out after everyone leaves, and invite her back to my place, and then…

"Maybe QA and support should all go for drinks one day," she says, a flush in her cheeks.

"I'd like that." I'm not sure how to interpret her invitation or the blushing, but I like that she wants to get together outside of work. Even if it is in a group.

Maybe she does like me back? I think?

She shifts on her little bunny feet.

"I should have known it was you in the costume," I say.

"What's that supposed to mean?"

"You're *such* a fresh-faced new girl. You've got hope in your eyes and joy in your heart. You haven't worked here for long enough to say no to things like this." I make a general motion to the bunny suit and the dead-eyed head under her arm.

She looks affronted. "I can say no!"

"No you can't. The fact that you're on the fun committee and dressed like a bunny right now proves it."

"*You're* on the fun committee."

Heat rises in my cheeks. I refuse to tell her why I'm on it. "And everyone else is either a keen newbie like you or HR," I say, dodging the confession.

"It's not my fault everyone else at the company is too boring to join."

"Not boring. Just wiser. Soon you'll realize that HR makes all of the decisions for events anyway. I don't know why we even have a committee. I guess it's to give the illusion that staff get a say."

"Oh my God, you're so jaded."

"Years of working in tech when you really want to be an artist will do that to a person."

"Staff totally get a say in events. Look at this awesome day we planned."

"The day *HR* planned. Name one idea that came from the rest of us that is actually being implemented today."

She opens her mouth, thinks for a long moment, then closes it.

"We're victims," I say firmly. "I never agreed to lead the bunny hop today, and I never agreed to hand out Valentine's Day chocolates while dressed like Cupid or host that virtual Scrabble party last month. But I did it, all because I'm on the fun committee."

All because of Jory, really.

"But you made a cute Cupid," she says, and drops her gaze and blushes deeper.

My heart leaps. Did she just call me cute? Oh my God, she thinks I'm cute.

"So, point taken, you hate this company and all manner of fun," Jory says.

I shush her, laughing in spite of myself. "You're going to get me fired."

"If you get fired, maybe you can use the severance pay to finally launch that art career," she says, cocking an eyebrow.

Wow. Ruthless.

"I'll—launch it once I—have more savings," I splutter. I hate it when people call me out for being too afraid to go after my dream. Because that's exactly what it is. And after our endless hours of messaging, Jory knows it.

She turns to the plastic table covered in extra gifts, chocolate, cups, our bags, and bits of plastic. "Ugh, I'm dying for some chocolate but I can't eat anything with this costume on."

She tries to grab a foil-wrapped egg with a bunny paw, and it slips from her fingers and hits the grass. I laugh.

"Here." I pick it up and unwrap it for her.

She opens her mouth.

I step forward and put it in her mouth—and the act is way more sensual than I was prepared for. She holds my gaze, and her lips brush my fingers as she takes it. A thrill goes through my middle.

We stand there. I should step back but I don't. I'm frozen in place, fluttery from the feel of her lips on my fingers.

And she's not stepping back either.

Then Jory makes a face. "Ew, I think some costume fluff got on the chocolate."

I laugh.

"Stop it. It's disgusting." She goes to wipe the fluff out of her mouth, looks at her paw, and moans. "This costume is the worst."

"Who's the fun-hater now?"

She tries to bat my nose, and I flinch away.

"Don't touch me with that," I say, laughing. "The bunny suit freaks me out."

"I noticed." She casts me a teasing smile. "What, you don't like giant fuzzy paws touching your face?"

She reaches for me, wiggling her fingers, and I back away with my hands out defensively.

"Don't you dare," I say—but my playful tone gives me away.

She puts the bunny head on the table with a mischievous expression, then advances on me with both paws up. "Hide your kids, hide your wife."

"You're ruining the Easter bunny for the children!" I back into the corner of the tent, trapped. She closes in and rubs the fuzzy paws over my face, not letting me escape. And secretly, or maybe not so secretly, my heart is doing flips. I fend her off, and she responds by trying to tickle me.

"You don't know who rented this costume before you or what kinds of things they touched with those paws!" I say, maybe a little too loudly.

We struggle, giggling, until I win by grabbing her wrists. Nose-to-nose, we catch our breath, and I can smell the sweet chocolate I just fed her. She's flushed and clammy, and I'm prickling worse than ever beneath my sweater. I think the temperature just went up ten degrees in here.

I bite my lip. She gives me her signature little smile, which puts dimples in her cheeks and always makes me melt like a chocolate egg in the sun.

Footsteps get closer outside the tent, and Trish from HR shouts to someone about finding the photographer.

Jory and I step apart.

Trish pokes her head into our refuge. "Jory, it's picture time. Good, Emma, can you bring out the lights and backdrop?"

"Sure," Jory says cheerfully.

"Yep," I say, trying not to sound disappointed by the interruption.

Trish leaves, and the two of us plunge into silence.

Okay, the time is now. How can I ask out Jory while also not making things awkward at work if her answer is no? Even though she obviously likes me, we're coworkers, and dating a coworker is pretty much never a good idea. Asking her out could go very badly.

The safer option would be to do nothing. We would continue flirting and not dating, and I would continue pining. Forever.

But she's standing in front of me, her cheeks flushed, her hair a mess, smiling sheepishly in a way that makes my knees weak. There's no misinterpreting the way she's been acting around me. So I have to make a decision, one way or another.

She grabs the bunny head, ready to put it on.

"Jory, wait." My mouth is dry.

She stops. Her eyes are a little wide, like I've startled her. Does she know what's coming?

At the hesitation, she steps closer. "What?"

"Um—" I draw a steadying breath. The step closer is encouraging. Do I tell her I like her? Do I ask her how she feels? God, what words do I choose?

The silence has gone on for too long. She's searching my face, her brow furrowed.

"Do you want to go out sometime?" I ask, the words coming in such a rush that I'm not sure if they were intelligible.

There's a pause that seems to last forever. My heart stops.

Jory's face breaks into a wide smile. Somehow, even though she's in a ridiculous bunny suit that sometimes shows up in my nightmares, she looks gorgeous.

And then—I must be dreaming—she steps even closer.

She takes my hand in her bunny paw. And I'm not even creeped out by the feel of the fuzz against my palm.

We're a breath apart. She inclines her head.

My stomach swoops.

I lean in, and our lips touch in a gentle, silent kiss. She's soft, sweet, making me want more before it's over.

"Yes," she whispers, her breath tickling my lips.

My heart is doing the bunny hop. *Forward, back, hop, hop, hop.*

With a glint in her stunning brown eyes, Jory puts on the bunny head. She leaves the tent, leaving me staring after her.

I draw a shaky breath, my whole face stretching into a huge smile.

I guess it was worth joining the fun committee, after all.

The Mermaid in the Bering Sea

Lost in dangerous waters, a young woman reflects on missed opportunities, and meets someone who can change her life forever.

I survived the longest night of my life—and probably the last. The horizon has vanished beyond the ten-foot swells tossing me around, but somewhere between the waves and the gray clouds, the sun is rising.

I don't know how to feel about the piece of wood I've been clinging to. I love it for keeping me alive, I guess.

But I hate it for not being big enough that I can get my whole body onto it, and I hate it for being so unstable that water constantly crashes over it. Most of all, I hate it for giving me hope that I'll survive. I could be peacefully dead right now instead of bobbing through the angry Bering Sea with a raspy throat and no feeling in my limbs.

People have been lost at sea for months before being rescued, so two days isn't a long time to be adrift. But those people had water and food, and they were probably floating in the tropics.

Me? I'm in a sea so violent there's a TV show about it. Enormous waves bring me several feet up and down, crash over my head, and spin me like a top, testing the limits of my orange survival suit. I keep thinking I see someone—a flash of hair, the glint of a pair of eyes— but then it's gone, like a mirage.

I wonder if search and rescue can even get out here in the storm. I wonder how storms can form so quickly. I wonder what I would be doing today if I hadn't taken that fisher job.

"I wonder…" I whisper, the first words past my lips in hours.

My throat is painfully dry and salty.

Some deep survival instinct tells me to catch a fish or a bird and drink its blood. But even if I had the strength and tools for that, what's the point? The freezing temperature will kill me anyway.

A wave crashes over top of me, leaving me gasping. I can't take this anymore. I should let go of my raft and let it all be over.

But as much as my brain is telling me to let go, my body won't listen. I keep gripping the wood, unmoving. I don't want to die. I have to find a way to survive this.

I kick my weak legs even though I'm sure it doesn't help. The wind howls in my ears, thunder rolls in the distance, and after so long out here, the sounds of Mother Nature turn into a song.

I hum along to the tune of a sea shanty, making up the lyrics using my last two unfrozen brain cells.

"There once was a girl who went to sea,

To escape her life in a small city,

Her hopes were high and her dreams were big,

'Til a cyclone took her down…"

I knew this was a risk when I decided to become a fisher but I never thought it would happen to me—especially not a measly three months into my career. I was supposed to turn twenty-one next week, and the friends I made at work were going to take me to the bar.

Tears burn in my eyes, catching me by surprise.

Stop it. What's the point in crying?

I keep kicking, my legs growing weaker. As I search for the next verse of my shanty, even my brain is sluggish.

What rhymes with hopeless?

As a swell lifts me higher, something catches my eye.

A whale?

Crap, I'm about to get eaten by something that thinks I'm a seal.

No—it's a human head.

My heart jumps into my throat. Is this the body of a crewmate?

"You need help," she says, and it takes a long moment for the words to settle over me.

The head belongs to a woman. A very alive woman. She's looking at me from the waves with concern pinching her brow. Her deep brown skin glistens, and her teal eyes glow like the bioluminescent creatures that surrounded me in the coldest hours of the night. Her bone structure is sharp, with high cheekbones and a prominent clavicle. Her long, curly hair undulates on the surface. She's so beautiful that it's hard to look at her, like I'm gazing at something forbidden.

This must be the end. I'm hallucinating. My mind is playing one last game before it shuts down. Because in the middle of this icy nothingness, there is no reason for a woman to be out for a skinny dip.

We drift closer. I can't tell if she's swimming toward me or if my raft is floating in her direction.

"Where is your ship?" Her voice is accented, like English isn't her first language. Her tone is the most beautiful melody, cascading over me like a warm shower. I want to close my eyes and sink into it.

She's within arm's reach. If she's a hallucination, she's a very convincing one.

"Are you okay? Can you understand me?" she purrs, reaching up to touch me. Between my survival suit and my numb body, I can't feel her. But I see her hand press down on my upper arm, real, solid, glistening.

I blink to see her better, and my breath catches. I've never seen anything more lovely. I could gaze at her for hours.

"Are you real?" I ask, the words barely passing my dry throat.

Her lips curve into a little reassuring smile, and everything inside me calms.

She puts her hands on my raft to rise up next to me, and I catch the scent of her. She's sweet and earthy, like Mother Nature sent her to me from a place far away from humans.

As she rises from the water, my gaze lingers on her breasts, which are plump and round. I blush and avert my eyes, ashamed of the way my attention lingered.

And as I take in the rest of her, my heart flips.

Instead of legs, she has a thick, scaly, silvery-brown tail.

All the blood drains from my head. Dread fills my chest, suffocating.

"Sea demon," I gasp, trying to roll away. But there's no room to move, and I'm too weak to do more than flinch.

No wonder she's devastatingly gorgeous. The rumor is that they infest the Pacific Ocean, luring sailors with their supernatural beauty, drowning them, and eating them.

The mermaid shakes her head, her teal eyes widening. She isn't denying who she is—more like arguing with my reaction.

With the way she's gazing at me, her eyes full of kindness and gentle concern... I don't know what to believe anymore.

The mermaid pulls off my glove and entwines my hand in hers, and I'm so numb that I barely feel it. My hand is skeletal and gray.

"Have you made peace with death?" she asks.

A huge swell lifts us up to the heavens, then down into the deepest trough, and all the while, the mermaid grips my hand tightly.

I scoff. "No. I've barely lived."

As I look at our entwined fingers, tears burn in my tired eyes. I grip her tighter.

"I don't believe you," she says. "How did you end up here? By living, no?"

"But I haven't done what I want to do, or seen what I want to see, or..." So many regrets swirl around in my brain—and maybe it's this beautiful mermaid bringing one particular thought to the front, or maybe it was hovering there all along, but the first thing out of my lips is, "I let the girl I love go. She's married now, and I never even told her how I feel."

I wipe my other hand across my teary eyes, which makes my face even wetter.

"Why not?" the mermaid asks gently. She's closer, her sweet breath filling me. My lips tingle, and I fight the urge to run my fingers through her long hair and pull her face to mine.

This must be the allure. She's toying with me, seducing me with her magic, before she drowns me.

It doesn't matter. I'm going to die soon anyway.

"Because my parents wanted me to marry a man with a good job," I say, "have kids, buy a house in the suburbs…" My words dry up, and my throat is too tight to finish the sentence.

Instead, I spiraled around secret crushes on girls, hating my parents, wishing for an escape to a place where I would be accepted.

Beads of water drip down the mermaid's curly hair and roll over her shoulders. I study her strong arms and her delicate, feminine hands, and I can't deny this feeling of want in my heart. I love women, and I always have. I'm attracted to this mermaid in a way I've never felt with any man. But I've never been able to admit this, and now it's too late.

I draw a slow breath, and let it out in a huff. "The only decision I made for myself was when I moved to Alaska to take a job as a fisher. I snapped. I took the first job opening that would get me far away from my parents and anyone they expected me to marry. Look where that got me."

The mermaid is quiet for a moment. "Maybe you're here with me for a reason. Maybe you weren't meant to live on land, nor were you meant to do what your parents—"

A spark of anger rises in me. "You think I'm supposed to die today?"

"That's not what I meant." She pushes my hood back to comb her soft fingers through my hair. She caresses my face, and traces a finger along my lower lip.

Pleasure ripples through me, warm and blissful, like it's the only thing keeping me alive.

"Wait, you're the one who brought back my phone when I dropped it in the water," I say, drawing a sudden connection to that bewildering memory of finding my lost phone on the edge of the deck.

The mermaid's lips curve into a tiny smile.

"How long did you watch our ship?" I ask.

"I've seen you every day for two months."

My heart skips. So I've had a guardian angel all this time.

"I feel your aura," she says, her brow pinched as she traces a finger over my jawline. "Your heart is strong, and you're not ready to die."

"My heart isn't strong," I say, choking on the words. "I've lived in fear."

"That isn't true," the mermaid says, and her tone is so sharp that I shut up. "It takes a brave person to sail these waters."

"This isn't bravery. If I were brave, I would have lived differently. I would have let myself love who I love, and I would have told my parents to shove it long ago."

The mermaid looks at me so tenderly, with such understanding, that a lump forms in my throat. Like looking at the sun, I can't keep my gaze on her for long.

"Wanting to be accepted by your family doesn't make you weak," she says. "Being scared doesn't mean you're not brave."

"Then what does it mean?"

"It means you care. You care about your family, you care about others, and you care about your place in the world. You have so much love inside you that you put it before everything else, including your own happiness."

Her words make my chest tighten. I want to believe she's right. I don't want to reach the end of my life resenting myself for the choices I made and the fears I had.

"Well, I'm done with all of that," I say. "I'm done caring about what anyone else thinks. I'm done being scared. And—"

A smile tugs at the mermaid's lips. I meet her gaze, my heart flipping.

"And I think you're really beautiful and sweet, and if you were a person, I would ask you out," I say in a rush, and as the words pass my lips, my body feels lighter.

There. I did it. I admitted my feelings out loud.

And even though I might be about to die, I feel pretty good. At least I asked out one girl before I died.

Sort of.

Hypothetically asking out a mermaid will have to do.

The mermaid's smile widens, and she's so stunning that my breath catches. She lets out a little laugh that rings like a melody over the wind. "And my answer is yes."

I blink. "Yes? You mean you would go out with me?"

"Of course."

I didn't think she would answer. And I sure didn't think I was good enough to snag someone so gorgeous.

I smile back, the muscles in my face tight after spending so long not using them.

She leans in, and I can see every bead of water on her smooth face. My belly swoops.

Wait, is she going to kiss me?

Surprised, I lean back.

She touches a finger to my lips, something curious behind her eyes. It's like she's asking me a question.

"I can help you," she murmurs.

What is she on about? Is she trying to kiss me or save me?

"Do you want to live underwater?" she asks, and the question hovers over us, taking a long time to reach my brain.

"I…" My heartbeat quickens. "What do you mean?"

"I mean that mermaids have been turning lost sailors into merpeople for millennia. All it takes is a kiss."

My breath catches.

The mermaid kiss was supposed to be a myth. Stories of lost sailors turning up as merpeople are scattered around the globe but I never gave them a second thought.

My heart jumps. This is my hope of surviving.

"What if a helicopter comes for me?" My pulse is stronger, like my body is fighting for its last moments.

"If you want to wait for one, that is your decision."

"I..." I swallow hard.

The thing is, even if a helicopter comes, what do I have on land? What if everything I'm meant for is under the surface?

"What happens if I go with you?" I ask. "Where will I live?"

The mermaid slides a hand around the back of my neck, locking my gaze. A flutter fills my belly.

"I've known since I first saw you that you're who I've spent my life looking for," she says, and for the first time, something nervous crosses her expression. She swallows. "So if you can trust a stranger... I promise I'll stay with you."

My heart seems to swell. Her promise to support me even though she doesn't know me makes tears spring in my eyes all over again. Where has this sort of promise been my whole life? Why couldn't I get support from the people I needed it from?

"Trust has been a little hard for me," I say. "So I guess today's a good day to start."

All it takes is a kiss. And then I'm a mermaid. Forever.

If the mermaid is lying… Well, then at least I'll die having finally kissed a girl. I've wanted to since I was fourteen. I owe it to myself.

My life is about to end so what do I have to lose?

The mermaid must sense the change in me—my aura, as she said—because she smiles. She cups my face while catching her plump bottom lip on her teeth. I imagine running my tongue along her lips in a playful kiss, and I bite my own lip.

"I can take you into the sea with me," she says. "I can transform you right now. I just need you to tell me if you want to live or die today."

I open my mouth, and for a moment, I can't get any words out. My chest is tight, making it hard to breathe.

She looks at my throat, like she can see my pulse beating faster, and tilts her head.

"Yes," I whisper. "I want to kiss you, and I want to be a mermaid."

I lean in, sliding a hand around the back of her neck.

She leans in to meet me.

My insides erupt in a dance.

Our lips touch, and my breath catches. I'm so numb that I can't tell whether she's cold or warm, but I do know that she's sweeter than anything I've ever tasted. Our lips move gently at first, and then the kiss deepens.

I open my lips wider, inviting her in. Her tongue plays with mine, making me dizzy.

I don't know how long she has to kiss me in order for me to transform into a mermaid but I don't want this to end. I move my lips eagerly, wanting more of her, licking the salty ocean from her lips.

A little moan escapes me, and I pull myself closer. It's like her kiss is breathing life into me, giving me energy and warmth.

I run my hands down her waist, savoring the shape of her. I wrap a hand around her and hold her close, wishing for this moment to last longer—wishing I'd kissed a girl sooner.

She pulls back, and I hold my breath. There's a glint of red in her eyes that makes my heart flip.

Am I about to find out this was all a trick, and now she's going to drown me?

But she murmurs, "We need to take this off," and unzips my survival suit.

I let out a breath. "Okay."

Whether I turn into a mermaid or not, this is my last moment as a human, so there's no use in keeping the suit on. I wiggle out of it, and my black wool shirt and pants are damp. The wind is biting. Deadly.

And yet...

I can move better than before. I can sit up, move my arms, wiggle my legs. Am I stronger? Am I imagining that the world is sharper around me?

Everything is brighter, louder, crisper.

The mermaid lifts my shirt a little, peeking at my skin.

Greenish scales are appearing on my hips.

A laugh bubbles up inside me.

The mermaid smiles. "How do you feel?"

I kiss her again, my heart skipping. "Like I've just found something worth living for."

I might have just spent my last night as a human, but it's far from my last in this world. This is the first day of the rest of my life—one where I'm going to live for myself, and stop letting fear control me.

The mermaid takes my hand, and presses it to her lips.

As my body transforms, feeling rushes back into my limbs. The mermaid is warm, soft, and full of life. Hope courses through me, and with it, a rush of excitement for the new world I'm about to discover.

Call Me Blue

When a porter at a five-star hotel hits it off with a celebrity guest, she gets an invitation she can't refuse.

I smooth my black jacket, fix the angle of my cap, and plaster a smile on my face as the town car rolls to a stop in front of me. I open the back door, extending a hand to help the elderly man get out.

"Welcome to the Cedarwood, sir."

When you're a kid, everyone loves to ask you what you want to be when you grow up. My answer changed from year to year—dog trainer, teacher, bookshop owner, fashion designer.

I never guessed where I would end up at twenty-one years old.

I am the door person at a five-star hotel in downtown Vancouver. Not just any five-star hotel—this is the fanciest one in the city. Celebrities stay here, presidents and prime ministers stay here, and sometimes, locals do, just to say that they have.

My job is straightforward: greet guests as they arrive and depart, help them to and from their cars, make sure they don't get rained on, and otherwise do whatever they need me to do. At the Cedarwood, no matter who you are, you get treated as if you're the most important person ever to stay here.

It's not my dream career, but I don't know what my dream is so this will have to do for now. That's how I end up with all of my jobs—by asking myself what feels right for now.

"Enjoy your stay," I tell the elderly man, offering a bow as he walks past me into the lobby.

He nods and slaps a twenty into my palm.

The job has its perks.

I'm about to shut the door and return to my post when the glint of diamonds catches my eye across the lobby.

I stop breathing. Blue Rivers, action hero, queer icon, activist, and the most gorgeous woman I have ever met, is striding toward me. She's strong, tall, fair-skinned, with scarlet hair styled in loose waves, and dark eyes accented with smoky eye shadow. She's wearing a green suit that weakens my knees. The glint of diamonds is coming from a pendant settled deep in the V neck.

Everything about her is so perfectly put-together that her celebrity status is obvious at first glance. Normal people don't look or dress like this. Normal people aren't so stunning that they make me forget to breathe.

The elderly man and the smattering of other people in the lobby all turn their heads to watch her pass, not subtle about it.

A deep frown tugs Blue's features downward, but when she sees me, her face transforms. She casts me a dazzling smile, and by the time she's a stride away, my heart starts beating again. I open the door and let her through.

"Thank you, Tess," she says.

I grin back. Not everyone acknowledges me as they pass. Some people nod, some comment on how they don't often see a woman doing this job, and some get angry if I don't open the door exactly the way they would have liked me to.

But Miss Rivers... She smiles at me in a way that nobody has ever smiled at me. She calls me by my name, talks to me while she's waiting for her ride, asks me about my life, and tells me what's happened during her visit. She's been staying here for ten days, and I look forward to every time she comes and goes.

"H-how can I assist you, Miss Rivers?" I ask, tripping over my tongue. I step outside with her to stand on the curb, where she draws a deep breath of fresh air.

She stands strategically behind a planter, letting it block the passing pedestrians' view of her.

Her frown from a moment ago is lingering beneath the forced smile. If she were a friend, I would ask what's wrong. But she exists on an entirely different plane than me, so far from a friend that it's laughable for the word to even enter my mind.

"Honey, *please* call me Blue," she says, the same thing she's told me all week. Because she's so sweet and gregarious that I'm almost ready to believe that we are friends.

She touches my lower back, just for a second, and the sensation her hand leaves behind sends a wave of pleasure to my fingers and toes.

"Hey, the brunch you recommended yesterday was to die for," she says, standing close. "Thanks for that. But I'm not so sure about that seawall walk afterwards."

My gut twists with the realization that I might have led her astray. "Why not?"

"Five minutes into the walk, I almost got run over by an angry cyclist. Then it happened again a few minutes later."

I suppress a laugh. "By any chance were you walking in the bike lane?"

"There was a bike lane?"

I laugh. Her answering smile is so gorgeous that it knocks me off balance. God, I'm helpless around her.

"It's a nice park, though," she says. "So you still get a few points for that recommendation."

"Oh, good." I put a hand over my heart. "Okay, for today's recommendation, nothing close to a bike lane. How do you feel about tulips?"

Blue laughs. "Go on."

She cocks an eyebrow, irresistibly charming.

"Oh, you know what? Nevermind," I say with mock sadness. "There's a horse-drawn carriage at the tulip festival that you'd be a danger to. If you can't figure out a bike lane, I'd hate to see…"

"Hey!" She playfully flicks the cap on my head. It goes askew, and she reaches back up to reposition it gently atop my curls. "This looks super cute on you, Tess. The uniform. I like it."

My throat seems to close. It takes me a moment to choke out a response. "Thanks."

Talking to her like this—like we have been for the last few days—makes me wonder what would have happened if we'd met under any other circumstances. What if she were a normal person, and we'd met in a coffee shop?

I've been exploring different scenarios as I lay in bed each night, going over our conversations. It's easy to picture myself with her. Holding her hand. Making her laugh. Kissing her. Running my hands over her curves.

The way she's looking at me, biting her lip, I swear she can read my thoughts.

I clear my throat, forcing my mind away from that totally inappropriate place. "I actually used to work at that festival. And I can confirm that the horse carriages are far away from the pedestrians. So I think you'd be safe there."

She faces me fully. "You worked at a tulip festival?"

"Yeah. I drove one of the carriages."

Blue searches me with her dark eyes. "You're an interesting person, Tess."

Heat rises in my cheeks. Did the actual Blue Rivers just call me interesting?

I shrug. "I wouldn't say that. I'm just someone who can't make up her mind about careers."

Blue tugs her suit jacket and wiggles her shoulders, as if uncomfortable. "Tell me about it."

"What, you think about career changes?" I ask, surprised.

She tilts her head. "This life was chosen for me by my parents. Sometimes, I don't know how much I like it. It's stressful, tiring, and very lonely."

"I've heard it gets lonely." I study her, finding the layer of sadness beneath this perfectly put-together exterior. It's something about her posture—defeated— and the way her smile flickers between genuine and forced as she talks to me.

"What would you do instead?" I ask.

Blue's eyebrows pinch together as she looks at me, her gaze searching.

"I'm sorry," I say with a start, like I've been caught breaking the law. "I'm overstepping. Please don't let me hold you up. Would you like me to call for—?"

"I want to be a teacher," she says quietly. "Elementary school, I think."

I let out a breath, trying not to be so tense. She must think I'm uptight. "You'd be a good one. The kids would love you."

Blue opens her mouth, closes it, then looks straight ahead. My heart is beating fast for some reason.

A black car pulls up, and an older woman rolls down the rear window. Automatically, I step forward to help her get out.

"I'm not getting out," she barks, waving me off like a fly. "Hurry up, Blue. We're late."

She says this like it's Blue's fault.

Blue casts me an apologetic look as she walks to the other side of the car. I hurry after her to help her get in.

She stops me with a gentle hand on my wrist before I can open the door.

"What time are you done your shift?" she whispers, her breath tickling my lips.

"Um—" My heart stumbles. She smells minty and fresh, and my imagination goes to a place where I can taste her more thoroughly.

I feel like I shouldn't answer. Am I allowed to share details about my shifts? It's like there's an implied rule that guests should think of me as part of the hotel, not a human being with a life outside of this. But my lips move before I can stop myself. "Nine o'clock."

She nods. There's a pause. Standing an inch from me, she opens her mouth, and then turns to the car door.

No! What was she going to say? Why did she ask me when I'm off?

Remembering my duty, I jump forward to open the car door for her. She already has her fingers around the handle, so I end up grabbing her hand.

"Sorry. I'm sorry." My face is burning.

Her gaze catches on mine, and the faintest smile tugs at her lips.

She turns her hand, palm up, and laces her fingers through mine as if I'm helping her to get into the car. She holds my hand for longer than needed, her thumb making a little circle.

My head spins, my brain slow to process what's happening.

"Buckle up, and let's go," the woman beside her barks. "We've got lunch with Steven before the fitting, and he wants you to look at this script. Tell me what you think. I think it's trash but we might have to take it…"

"See you later, Tess," Blue murmurs, holding my gaze. Her eyes are pleading for help but I can't do a thing about it.

"Enjoy your day, Blue."

Her lips twist into a sad smile.

I wish I could whisk her back into the hotel, and we could order room service, watch movies, and float in the swimming pool all afternoon.

Instead, I shut the car door, and step back.

As the driver takes Blue away from me with that awful woman who must be her manager or publicist, I take deep breaths to calm my racing heart.

What was all of that about? Why did she take my hand, stand so close, and ask when I'm off?

It's absurd of me to even consider this, but... Is she flirting with me?

I smooth my jacket and return to my post. No, I'm being hopeful and jumping to conclusions. Blue Rivers isn't interested in me. She's my celebrity crush, and way out of my league.

I must be mistaking kindness for flirting. It's the only explanation.

* * *

At the end of my shift, I head to the staff lounge, where I change out of my uniform and gather my stuff at a snail's pace. Blue still hasn't returned, and by 9:15 p.m., I can't stall any longer. It's time to go home.

I'm about to head to the parkade when Nick at the front desk pokes his head into the staff lounge. "Tess, can you bring this up to room 2205? I just got a call, and she requested that you do it."

He's holding one of the complimentary toiletry bags we give to all guests.

My heart skips. "Blue Rivers?"

"Yeah. I don't know why she asked for you specifically. Or why she needs this. Celebs are weird."

"She wants me to bring this to her room?"

"Yes," he says slowly and clearly. "Room 2205."

I take the embroidered rose-gold bag and master key, and walk to the elevators in a daze. On the ride up, I check my reflection. My white lace top is sitting nicely, my wide-leg jeans are as cute as ever, and my boots are dirt-free. I look tired from the long shift, so I rummage in my bag for makeup. A dusting of powder helps. I have time to take out my bun and set my curls free before the elevator door opens.

My feet move on their own as I walk down the hall.

Room 2205.

My heart is hammering against my ribs.

I knock. Nobody answers, of course. She hasn't returned yet. I let myself inside, and put the toiletry bag on the bathroom counter.

God, this suite is gorgeous. Everything glistens, and there are crystals embedded in the floor.

I chew my lip. Was that all Blue wanted? Am I overthinking this? I should leave before she gets back. I could get fired if someone finds out I'm lingering in a guest's room.

And then there's the fact that I'm here because I must think there is some chance that Blue Rivers is interested in me. As if she would be interested in a porter. There's no reason a well-established celebrity would be into a girl who can't even figure out what she wants to do with her life.

Ugh, what am I doing? I have to get out of here.

I make for the door, my pulse racing. If I can go down the stairs, maybe I won't run into her in the elevator.

My hand is on the knob when the lock clicks. I gasp, my hand automatically going to my heart.

The door opens, and Blue Rivers steps inside.

"Hi," I say in a rush. "I was just— I brought you— I'm sorry I'm still in here."

Blue shuts the door and walks past me, not meeting my eye. For an absurd second, it's like I'm invisible. Then she puts her purse on the TV stand, and faces me.

"This is my last night here." There's a flash of something new in her expression. Is that nervousness?

I absorb her words, and my heart sinks. "Oh. I've liked talking to you during your stay."

She reaches behind her neck to unclasp the diamond pendant, and my gaze drops to it deep in her cleavage before she takes it off and sets that down, too. She steps closer to me. "Same."

My breath catches. If she steps any closer, I might lose strength in my knees.

"Talking to you earlier made me realize a few things," she says. "First, that I want to take more control over my career. Second... Um, remember what I said about one of the problems with this life?"

"That it's stressful and... lonely?" I say, my mouth dry.

She nods. Swallows. Her gaze traces over me from my hair to my boots. "You looked hot in the uniform, but I think I like you in normal clothes even better."

Hot? She thinks I'm hot?

I try to thank her but I can't get any words out.

"Tess…" She seems to struggle with what to say next, biting her lip.

Something inside my chest erupts, making it hard to breathe. "What did you have in mind for tonight?" I whisper.

She's so close that I can smell the sweet, strawberry scent on her lips. "Hmm… Is there anything you would like to do?"

My lips tug into a smile. "I can think of a few things."

She leans in.

And finally, with a wave of cool relief, I can't deny what's happening for another second.

I close the distance, lifting my hands to her hair.

Our lips meet, and I'm surprised by the heat of the kiss. We both move eagerly, our breaths coming fast, our lips and tongues quick. I'm so lightheaded that I'm sure I would have lost my balance if she weren't holding me firmly against her. Her hands run through my curls, sending a shiver through me.

I part her lips with my tongue, tasting her, and she's as sweet as I imagined—like a strawberry smoothie. It makes me moan, and I kiss her deeper.

Her hands are firm as they wander over the bare skin at my waist, sending a ripple of pleasure low inside me.

I let my fingers roam down her suit. It's softer than I'd imagined. I hook my fingers into the deep V, and she lets out a breath. I unbutton it carefully—it's probably more expensive than everything I own.

We undress each other, our fingers fumbling with all the zippers and buttons. She turns my shirt and jeans inside out. I try to remove her suit more carefully, but she hisses, taking over to shrug out of it and drop it on the floor.

I'm frozen in place as I take in Blue's gorgeous body. I've seen her half-naked in movies before but this is so different. This is real.

She pushes me onto the bed, and climbs on top of me. She kisses my neck, chest, and leans down to suck my nipples. I gasp, making fists in her hair.

We explore each other's bodies with our hands and mouths, experimenting with what makes each other gasp. I'm dizzy, wet, aching for more.

I roll us over before she can resist, making her laugh. Spread beneath me, her red hair tangled across the pillows, she casts a teasing half-smile. Seeing that expression on her is enough to make my insides burn with need.

I graze my fingers gently down her stomach. She moans, parting her legs for me.

I bite my lip, making myself go slowly.

"You tease," she whispers, closing her eyes. "The number of times I imagined bringing you up here this week…"

She grabs my hips, holding me close.

"I can't tell you how glad I am that you did," I murmur into her neck.

Her hand wanders low, and when she slides a finger between my legs, I gasp, my eyelids fluttering shut.

I glide two fingers between her folds, savoring the way she trembles beneath me. I kiss her lips softly, stifling her moans, and I can't help rocking my hips as she rubs between my legs. I get lost in her, forgetting where we are, and forgetting all of the reasons why I thought this would never happen.

Her hand moves faster, and her breaths become hitched, and my gentle kisses on her neck and shoulders turn into nips.

"Close?" I murmur.

"Yeah," she says, the word a whimper.

"Same."

Our fingers quicken, our hips rock, and Blue cries out, trembling. Her ecstasy tips me over the edge, and I gasp, climaxing with her. I lose strength in my arms as the waves of pleasure overtake me, the sensation so intense that I can't help crying out. My mind seems to disconnect from my body in a long moment of bliss.

As we come down, I roll off her, catching my breath. We're both sweaty. Her hair is a tangled mess, and it's a beautiful sight.

Gazing at the crystal ceiling, I murmur, "I can't believe you get to stay in hotels this nice. Maybe if I actually picked a career and stuck with it, I could afford to stay somewhere like this one day instead of just working here."

Maybe. I'm saying the words but I don't believe them. I like trying odd jobs. It's possible that my dream job is exactly what I'm doing.

Besides, if I'd picked a conventional career and stuck to it, I probably wouldn't be naked with Blue Rivers right now.

I meet her gaze again.

She lifts a shoulder. "It's all superficial. Who cares about chocolates on the pillow and complimentary slippers? None of that matters."

I shuffle around to face her, propped up on one hand. "What does matter?"

She searches my face, a little smile tugging at her lips. "People. Experiences. Nights like this."

I lean in and kiss her full lips, my heart expanding.

Whatever happens from here, she's right. This was a night I'll never forget.

Cacti and Crystals

At the farmers market, Olivia sets up her booth next to her infuriatingly attractive nemesis.

It's a perfect day for a farmers market, and Ember had better not ruin it for me. Throngs of customers stroll through the booths with their wallets ready while the hot sun beats down on us. A live band is setting up across the park, sure to lure in more people.

"Thanks so much for your purchase, ma'am," I say, helping my customer put her potted succulents into a box. It's not even ten and I've already sold six plants. This bodes well.

"Seems like everybody I know has these little cactus things," the lady says. "You should see how many my granddaughter has. Not a clear spot on any of her windowsills!"

I cast her a charming smile. "Plants are the new pets, as they say."

She laughs. "Well, I'll take good care of my new pets."

She walks away with her purchase, looking pleased.

From the booth beside me, Ember snorts.

Anger licks through me. Somehow, they always end up next to me at these markets. I need to have a word with whoever designs the booth layout. Why can't I be placed next to someone cool with an actual useful product? A bakery, maybe?

Instead, I get to sit next to a table full of rocks.

Sorry, not rocks. *Crystals* and *gemstones*. Call them rocks and Ember will shoot you a glare fiery enough to melt them all.

Ember is finishing setting up, which gives me a rush of satisfaction.

"You're late," I say, sliding my chair further into the shade. My red tank top and booty shorts offer minimal coverage, and my freckled skin is too pale to handle more than a few minutes of sun. I let my hair down and try to fan it out over my shoulders for extra protection.

"Some of us have lives outside of this, Olivia," Ember says, returning my snippy tone. They scrutinize me as I run my fingers through my brunette locks.

"Well, while you were off living life, the rest of us were making sales," I say smugly.

And I'm determined to keep it up. I have to sell more than Ember today so I can rub it in their face.

Ember ignores this, and plunks down in a folding chair.

They're dressed in flowy orange pants with an obnoxious floral pattern, and a teeny tiny tassel crop top that reveals a lot of midriff. It's a shame to see such devastatingly good looks wasted. I can't deny that they're attractive, with their black pixie cut, brown skin, bold eyebrows, cute nose piercing, and nicely shaped lips. Not to mention that kissable jawline. But their personality totally ruins it.

A young couple slows down to peer at the rocks, and Ember flashes a smile. "Morning!"

The first time we met, Ember had the nerve to tell me my booth was unethical and bad for the environment. I snapped back that I use biodegradable pots instead of plastic, source my plants ethically, and plants consume carbon dioxide and toxins. But I guess my arguments weren't good enough because there's been friction between us ever since.

A teenage girl with pale skin, waist-length brown hair, and a half-eaten scone in her hand stops at Ember's booth. "Do you have selenite?"

Ember reaches across the table for a white crystal. "Yes, right here."

"My friend told me it helps create positive energy flow?"

"It does. If you put one in four corners of your house, it'll create a positive energy circuit."

I roll my eyes.

"Cool! I'll take four," the girl says. "Mom?"

Her mom comes over with her credit card ready.

"I've got plants," I say. "These ones are two for ten. Scientifically proven to reduce the harmful toxins in your house."

Ember glares at me as the girl and her mom shuffle over to my booth.

Minutes later, the pair walks away with two plants from my table, and a bag of rocks from Ember's table.

"Do you honestly believe all of that energy circuit stuff?" I ask Ember.

Ember narrows their eyes. "Why would I be here selling them if I didn't?"

We pause our argument to smile at a passing family.

"Why does it have to be moonlight that charges the stones?" I ask. "Can't I put it under a lamp?"

Ember's scowl deepens. "The idea is to charge them in nature. The moon, water, soil—"

"Water? So I can charge it in the kitchen sink?"

They pick up a jet-black stone, walk over to slap it down on the edge of my table, and return to their folding chair.

I open my mouth, then firmly close it.

Don't give them the satisfaction of asking. Ignore them.

Ember waits, holding my gaze with their luminous green eyes.

It's not often you meet people with eyes that green. Or bright.

It's hard to hold their gaze for long, so I look back at the crowd.

A pair of young women steps up, sparing me from this silence.

"Morning!" I say. "What sort of plants are you looking for today?"

While I tell them about which plants thrive in which conditions, I overhear snippets of Ember's conversation with a customer.

"Yep, you'll want to look at rose quartz or morganite for that…"

I tell my customers about the benefits of having an aloe plant.

"Obsidian?" Ember says loudly. "Yeah, that's perfect if you have toxic people and want to ward off their negative energy." They step over to my table to pick up the rock they put there—and I swear they raised the volume of their voice on purpose.

I scoff, and Ember must hear it because they glance my way before returning their attention to the customer.

"Let me put these in a box for you," I tell the two young women, and carefully place their purchases into a tray.

They leave, but I don't get the chance to bask in victory because Ember's customer leaves with a purchase too.

"Why are you so determined not to believe in crystals, Olivia?" Ember asks me.

A small smile threatens to show on my lips. Something about the way they say my name is nice. But I tamp down that thought. "There's nothing to *believe*. It's just facts. You can't *charge* a rock, they don't emit energy that has an effect on us, and they can't heal us. They're just pretty to look at. Like, I'm sure the placebo effect is strong, and if you think they work for you, great—but they don't do anything themselves. Taking peoples' money for rocks is dishonest."

"I'm not tricking anybody into anything. They come to me willingly. But what makes you so sure that they don't do anything? Don't you think it's possible that the chemical composition of something can have an effect on us, the same way unseen things like radiation do?"

"I'm a scientist, Ember. Or, I will be. I'm studying chemistry at university."

Ember's lips quirk. They search my expression with a hint of curiosity. "I'm going to university too."

"Really?"

"Business, of course." They flourish at the rocks—as if it's obvious that this sort of thing requires a business degree. "So as a chemist, you should understand that the makeup of everything on this planet is more complex than it looks, and it's possible that crystals and gemstones can have an effect on us."

There's a pause.

"Which university do you go to?" I ask.

"Portland State."

"Are you serious? Me too."

There's something gentler in Ember's expression. When they're not scowling at me, their face becomes softer, more captivating. It sparks something in my midsection, which I ignore.

"Why are you taking chemistry when you run a successful plant business?" Ember asks, raising a perfect eyebrow.

I hesitate, not sure whether I want to get into it with them. But something I can't identify makes me open my mouth and confess. "This isn't really what I want to do. I inherited this business from my mom. She passed away a few years ago. I didn't want to let the business drop so I kept it going. But I think I'd rather get a degree. I don't know. That's just how I feel."

"Oh," Ember says, leaning back. "I'm sorry to hear about your mom."

"Thanks."

"You okay?"

"Better as time passes, I guess. I feel connected to her when I run the booth. I'm lucky that I'm able to do this and go to school. It's a good weekend job."

"Yeah, totally."

The air feels a little lighter. I shift in my seat, not sure where to look. Suddenly, I'm self-conscious under their gaze.

More customers step forward, and I let out a breath of relief at the opportunity to stop talking about this. I don't know why I spilled all of that—and to Ember, of all people.

In the next lull, Ember turns back to me, angling their whole body.

That's new. Normally, we angle away from each other in disgust.

"Why are you never at the farmers market at the university?" Ember asks.

Another question with a doozy of an answer. I guess I'm two feet into personal confessions now. I sigh. "My ex-girlfriend helps run it, along with… um, her fiancée. Getting a booth there means talking to them, and nothing in the entire universe is worth that."

Ember stares at me for a long time—so long that I reach over to grab a random crystal and drop it in their lap.

"Here," I say. "It looks like you need to be recharged."

To my surprise, they laugh.

It's a cute look on them. Their whole face lights up.

"Are you in a relationship now?" they ask.

What? Where did that come from? Is it because I mentioned my ex?

"No," I say, eyeing them.

They nod. "Hm."

We hold each other's gaze. Around us, the crowd is thickening and growing louder as more people arrive.

"I was late today because my cat is sick," Ember blurts, fidgeting with the tassels on their tiny crop top.

Something heavy seems to sink into the pit of my stomach. "Oh. Crap. I'm sorry."

"He's at the vet today on IV. He'll be okay. Probably needs to be on meds for the rest of his life though."

"How old is he?"

"Five."

I nod. My heart gives a squeeze. "I have a cat too. I'd be a mess if she got sick. I'm so sorry."

"Thanks."

"Well, we're going to have to work extra hard to sell a lot of rocks—gems—crystals—to pay for that medication," I say with an awkward half-smile.

Ember returns my smile. "I guess we do. Now, sit back and watch me make more sales than you today."

I gasp in mock outrage. "Oh, it's on."

Something changes between us as we help a few more customers. I'm not sure why Ember told me that their cat is sick but it makes me hate them less. Who hates someone with a sick cat? I'm not a monster.

Maybe my confessions helped soften them up a little.

I kind of like it. This is easier than hating each other.

As we chat to passers by, my attention keeps pulling to the booth beside me. I wonder which part of town Ember lives in. I wonder how their business degree is going… and what their social life is like… and whether they're dating anyone.

Heat floods my face. Okay, I have to stop thinking about them now. This is ridiculous.

I should put in a request to be in a different spot next weekend. Setting up my booth next to Ember's is clearly distracting. I'm spending more time talking to them and thinking about them than with my customers.

"Hey, Olivia, I did some research last week," Ember says, suddenly looking uncomfortable. They shift in their creaky folding chair. "Um, I guess not all succulents are bad. Especially if you source them ethically. So… I wanted to apologize. For what I said when we first met."

I blink. "Oh. Um, thank you."

An awkward silence descends between us. This apology is nice to hear, to be honest.

"Well, I admire you for making a business out of rocks," I say, and then cringe. I can do better. "There are a lot of mysteries in the way the world works. The way chemicals and energy affect us is one of them. I guess we don't know for sure how certain crystals might affect us, and… I should be more open to that possibility."

Ember nods, a little smile tugging at their lips.

God, they really are cute.

Something is twisting inside me. Confusion? My entire relationship with Ember has been based on mutual resentment. Now what? Where does this put us if we're going to stop openly insulting each other's business?

As the farmers market wraps up, Ember slaps another stone on my table. It's opaque white.

I raise an eyebrow.

"White jade," they say. "Consider it a gesture of peace. Also…"

They rummage in their messenger bag, and pull out a green pen. I watch, my heart beating faster, as they write a phone number on the back of one of their business cards.

They step close, and my stomach swoops.

"Text me. If you want," they say. "Maybe I can take you out for dinner sometime."

I take the card numbly. Our fingers brush, and my heart stumbles over itself.

Seriously? Ember is asking me out?

We've never stood so close before, and it's doing something to me. They smell delicious, like vanilla and cinnamon. My gaze traces along their sharp jawline, and I swallow hard.

They step back, breaking the thread of tension.

As many weekends as we've spent arguing… and as much as they drive me crazy… there's something like a celebration going off inside my chest.

Because, fine, I've enjoyed our verbal sparring. And I've enjoyed spending time next to Ember every weekend.

And when I let myself go there… I would really like to kiss them. I want to run my lips along their jawline, wrap my hands around their waist, and pull them into a passionate kiss that snaps all of the tension that's been building between us for weeks.

I pick up the white jade, a smile tugging at my cheeks. "Cool. I will. I'd like that very much."

Ember grins back. And I swear, I can feel the white jade's energy making me a little bit warmer.

Leap of Faith

*As Kris tries to summon the bravery to leap off a rope swing,
her crush comes by to help her get past her fear, and makes a
tantalizing promise.*

I scramble up the muddy slope, my hands and knees
getting covered in grit. The hot sun dips lower in the sky,
and I have about an hour before it sets.

An hour to stop being such a wimp.

I can do this.

My heart is beating out of my chest, and not from the
hike through the forest to get here. I'm trembling as I
step out to the edge of the rock, gripping with my toes as

if that'll stop me from falling. Every step takes me closer to the bane of my existence: the rope swing suspended over the glassy lake.

I wipe my muddy hands on my butt, then regret it. Maybe this wasn't the best day to wear a white bikini.

With a steadying breath, I grab the curved stick that everyone uses to pull the rope closer. The stick has been rubbed smooth from all the handling, and stinks like sweat.

Gross.

"Carpe diem," I whisper like a meditation chant. "Carpe diem, carpe diem."

It's not helping. As much as I want to seize the day and experience the same adrenaline rush as everybody else who's ever been to this damn campground, I'm teetering on the edge of what is literally a cliff, holding onto an ancient rope, which is tied to a tree that's probably had enough of everyone's shit.

Is this safe?

I study the water as if expecting a hazardous boulder to have appeared since the last time someone did this. The water is dark with patches of weeds and lily pads across the surface. Will my legs get tangled? And does anything live in this lake?

I'm ten feet up but it feels like a hundred. The cliff looks so much higher from here than it did from the water.

There's a distant whoop. Across the lake, the five tiny figures of my friends watch me. They're warm and dry right now, and I hate them more for it. All of them did this swing earlier without hesitating. They did it several times.

Me? I stood back with my pulse racing, light-headed, feeling worse by the second for being such a wimp.

But I've had all afternoon to think, and I've decided I won't go home tomorrow without having done this. Today is the first day of a new Kris. A brave Kris.

I hold the rope with both hands, breathing deeply.

Is this whole carpe diem thing supposed to be so terrifying?

Footsteps approach from the forest.

Crap.

I let go of the rope and turn around, crossing my arms to shield my half-nakedness—which is ridiculous. We're at a lake, so of course I'm in a bikini.

The person looks up, and my insides flip over. I drop my arms, trying to look less awkward. Of course it's Faith. She and her friends are staying in the campsite next to us, and she's the type of woman who makes me forget how to say words. She's a little older than me, maybe in her early twenties, with an Australian accent that makes my knees weak. She's tan-skinned with brown eyes and long, brunette hair that she keeps down and messy under a backwards snapback hat. In the three days I've known her, she always looks like she's ready to go longboarding—today, she's in an oversized tee and board shorts. Everything about her is cooler than I will ever be, making me wonder why she bothers talking to me.

And now she's here to witness me being too afraid to jump off a little rope swing.

"Hey," I say weakly, offering a small wave.

Faith's face lights up with the most gorgeous smile. "I haven't missed the big jump?"

"Nope."

She kicks off her shoes, and scrambles up the slippery bank toward me.

What's she doing here? And why is she by herself?

"Did you get the sudden urge to jump?" I ask, motioning to the rope.

"Your friends sent me here."

"Oh."

I am absolutely going to murder them.

I look over to the campsite, where they're too far away to glare at, but I swear they're huddled together and watching us intently.

Last night, after darkness fell and the drinking games started, I spent more time talking to Faith than I did to my own friends. They teased me about it this morning, making me blush until I was so red that it looked like I had a sunburn. I guess I wasn't subtle about how much I like her—and if I was reading her correctly, I don't think she was subtle either. It was the way she spent all evening standing close, reaching out to touch my arm, leaning in under the pretense of getting closer to hear me better... She'd been such a tease. I'd wanted the night to end with her on top of me, but that sort of thing is a little hard when you're sharing a tent with other people. So between that and my being too shy to make a move, nothing happened. And I've spent all day regretting it.

"Afraid of heights?" Faith asks, standing next to me to gaze out at the lake.

I look uneasily at the water below. "I've never really thought about it. But… there's a small chance that I am."

She laughs. "I know your friends sent me here to pressure you, but Kris, at the end of your life, it won't matter whether you jumped off this rope swing or not."

"Won't it? I thought everyone on their deathbed says they regret not seizing the day more."

"Well, yeah, but there's a difference between seizing the day and giving into peer pressure." She shrugs. "Don't do it if you don't want to."

Her moral support is sweet. My lips tug into a smile. "It's not just pressure making me want to do this. I really want to."

"Yeah?" She nudges me gently, sending a tingle through my arm. "Why?"

"Because…" I search for words. The reason is solid in my head but I haven't explained it out loud to anyone. "I've spent my whole life with the reputation of being the reserved one. The quiet one. Like, when people meet my group of friends—" I point across the lake where they're still waiting for me to jump. "—I'm just a sidekick. An extra."

"Kris, that isn't true."

Something about the way she's looking at me makes my cheeks burn. Her lips curve upward, and they're full, shapely, pink… and so kissable.

I avert my gaze, aware that I'm staring at her lips. "It is. But I'm changing that. I want to be more outgoing so I made it my goal to carpe diem."

She faces me. "I like how quiet and thoughtful you are. I have five obnoxious siblings, and growing up, my house was never peaceful. Meeting you has been a breath of fresh air. You listen to me when I talk. You think about what you're going to say before you say it. You're introspective, I guess. It's cool. I like it."

I hold her dark gaze, her words sending a ripple of warmth through me. "I remember you said something last night about having fist-fights with five siblings."

"I did?" She grimaces. "Damn, I was so drunk, I don't even remember."

"Oh." Crap, does she remember we flirted? Was she flirting just because she was drunk? Maybe she isn't interested in me. The warmth from a moment ago dissolves.

"When did you set that goal?" Faith asks, pulling me out of my inward panic.

"Um—last week. It was my nineteenth birthday."

"Happy birthday." She's standing so close that I can feel her breath on my cheeks, and it's doing something to me. My insides are swooping all over the place.

I swallow hard. "Thanks."

"So you want to seize the day more? Did you feel like you weren't doing that before?"

I shake my head. "It was always just... school, softball, volleyball. Volunteering for credit, work experience, whatever. I like those things but my life has been a routine. I do everything for other people."

"Hm." Her dark eyes trace down my body, then back to my face. "What does your goal involve?"

"Like, doing one thing a day that scares me, being adventurous... you know." I'm losing the ability to form words again. What is it about her that makes me light-headed?

But I don't know if she's just standing close because the rock doesn't offer much room for both of us. There's a chance that I spent the whole weekend overestimating her attraction to me.

"What if that didn't have to involve adventurous and scary things?" she asks.

I furrow my brow. "Isn't that the point?"

"I think the point is to make each person seize the day in a way that means something to them. I'm sure not everyone gets joy out of the exact same things."

I squint at her, not sure where she's going with this.

"Like, is someone who goes out for a nice dinner seizing the day less than someone who goes skydiving?" she asks. "Even if the first person doesn't have any interest in skydiving?"

"Maybe? No? Fine, you're probably right." I bite my lip. I don't know where this leaves me. She's making me question my entire birthday goal—but I kind of like it. She has a way of making me rethink everything. Like last night when she asked me why I play volleyball.

Because... I just do? I like it, I think?

Honestly, being the quiet and introspective girl that I am, I like that about her. Our conversations don't stay on the surface for long.

Faith tilts her head, looking at me curiously. The way she stands so tall and confidently, I could melt into her arms. It would be so easy to sidle up next to her and let her drape her arm across my shoulders.

We should get dinner sometime and talk about this more, I want to say. But my face heats up, and my throat closes before I can open my mouth. Why do I have to be a giant chicken about absolutely everything in my life?

"Well, I'm still going to jump off this swing," I say. "Consider it part of my personal growth."

Faith laughs. "I can respect that."

She looks to where the sun is about to cross the horizon. It's cooler out than it was a few minutes ago. The fire back at the campsite is starting to sound really nice.

"I'll go first so you can see how easy-peasy it is." She winks, and my knees weaken.

As she walks past, she extends a hand to brush my waist.

My breath catches. A tingling sensation rushes through my midsection as she takes her hand away.

"Sure," I stammer. "Go for it."

Faith's lips pull into a suave smile. "Or do you want to go first and get it over with?"

My pulse picks up again. Dammit. I don't want to be this scared. "You go," I say casually. I square my shoulders and stand taller, hoping the feigned confidence turns into actual bravery.

She chews her lip, studying me. "You genuinely want to do this?"

I nod. "It's my Everest."

She grins. "Okay."

I step aside and lean against the tree, giving her space to run and jump.

She takes off her hat, pulls her t-shirt over her head, and takes off her shorts, and it's a good thing I'm leaning against a tree because I lose all feeling in my limbs. Her bikini is an athletic style that shows off how fit she is, and the bottoms are so revealing in the back that I have a heart attack as she turns around to put her clothes down.

Holy shit. I want her badly.

She uses the stick to pull the rope closer, then wraps her fingers around it, backing up. "Tell you what. I'll go, and you go immediately after me. No thinking, no hesitating. And when you land in the water… I'll give you a kiss."

A kiss? I'm still absorbing Faith's words when she runs off the cliff and swings through the air. She's suspended for a long moment, and then hits the water with a gentle splash.

There's a wild flutter inside me like birds flapping around in my chest and belly.

She surfaces, and wipes her hands across her eyes. She's wearing the same exhilarated, self-satisfied grin as everyone else who's jumped off this thing. It's a beautiful look on her.

"I'm holding you to your promise," I shout.

I grab the rope as it swings back to me, and grip it tightly, walking backward.

Is sex the world's best motivator? Because now, more than ever, I feel like I'm actually going to do it.

I'm doing it.

It's happening.

"Carpe diem," I whisper, and start running.

Every sensation is amplified as I run to the edge of the rock—the grit beneath my bare feet, the scratchy rope on my hands, the cool evening air biting my skin. My heart is going to pound out of my chest. There's a swoop inside me as I take off.

And then I'm airborne. I let out a whoop, and for a couple of seconds, I'm weightless. Faith cheers, her voice filling the still air. I think I can hear an eruption of cheers from the campground across the way.

I hold my breath as I hit the water, and my body kicks and flails automatically. I swim upwards, and my head breaks the surface.

"Yes!" I cry, wiping water from my eyes. "I can do anything!"

Faith laughs. I laugh with her, a celebration going on inside my chest.

I can't believe I did it. For a minute, I thought I would chicken out again and slump back to my friends in defeat.

Faith kicks backward, heading for the shore, holding my gaze. She's moving to the opposite side of the rock— where the campsites won't be able to see us, maybe?

I frog-kick after her, my heart now pounding for a totally different reason.

She sits at the edge of the lake, leaning against the shore, that suave smile on her lips.

I swim up to her, stopping at her knees. "How about that promise?"

It's probably the boldest thing ever to come out of my mouth, and I silently thank the rope swing for giving me the confidence to say it.

Faith leans forward, her elbows on her thighs, as smooth as hell. "I think you earned it."

I pull myself closer, rising from the water on my knees, and I'm right between her legs. With the rock jutting out between us and the campsites, the whole world becomes just us and the lake. Birds sing overhead, the trees stand still, and the water reflects the sky and shoreline like a mirror. The evening couldn't be more perfect.

I lean in until I'm close enough to see beads of water running down her face.

Her breath hitches.

I close the distance, pressing my lips gently to hers. An exhilarating tingle rushes through my face and down my body. She tastes like summer—warm, sweet, tropical.

She kisses me back, opening her lips, and it's everything I've been aching for all weekend. I place one hand on her thigh and the other on her cheek. Beneath the beads of cold lake water, her skin is hot.

Our lips move faster, the kiss deepening. She holds me with the same suave confidence that she showed on the rock, and it's turning me to putty in her arms.

I smile into her lips. "Thanks for coming out here to motivate me to jump," I murmur.

"Anytime." She kisses me harder, sliding her hands around my waist to pull me close.

A victory dance is happening in my midsection. I trace my palms up her soft thighs, wanting more of her.

She leans back on her elbows, and I follow her, our bodies pressed together on the shoreline.

As the sun sets over the lake, it hits me what I've all done today—not just conquering the rope swing, but summoning the courage to kiss the most beautiful, captivating woman I've ever met. I can't help smiling as I rock against her, savoring this perfect moment.

Maybe I do have some bravery in me.

An Honest Mistake

A mistaken transaction turns an embarrassing situation into an exciting second-chance romance.

"I made a really bad mistake," I shout into the phone, my heart beating fast. I pace my apartment, doing laps around the coffee table. Meadow watches me curiously from the top of her scratching post, her calico tail swishing.

"Miss, I need you to calm down," Veronica says on the other end, deadpan. She's the receptionist at Feline Pawadise, the cat rescue organization where I got Meadow.

I take a deep breath but it doesn't make me any calmer. "Look, I just submitted a donation on your website. It was supposed to be for a hundred dollars. But you know how the form shows dollars and cents?" I wave a hand at my laptop as if she can see me.

"I'm not familiar with how our donation form works," Veronica says way too calmly. "Dan runs the website. Do you want me to put you through to him?"

"What? No!" I cry. "Although Dan needs to be shouted at because that donation form is terrible. I swear I added an extra zero-zero for cents but—"

I rub a hand over my face. I'd meant to donate a hundred.

$100.00.

And yet, after I clicked submit, what did the donation receipt say?

$10000.

I don't know where I went wrong. I must have added the zeroes in the wrong box. Now an amount of ten thousand dollars is about to go through on my credit card.

If I ever meet this *Dan* person, I'm going to throttle him.

"I need to refund the donation I just made. I entered the wrong amount," I say, collapsing onto the couch. The worn-out upholstery engulfs me like a much-needed hug.

"You want to refund your donation to a charity?" Veronica asks flatly, judgment dripping from her tone.

My face heats up. "I want to donate, but not *that* much. I can't afford that. I'm probably going to get a call from the credit card company soon."

"Okay. I'll put you through to Devi. She handles our donations and accounting. What's your name?"

I sit taller, struggling with the couch. "Thank you. It's Sarah Chow."

"Please hold."

Tinny hold music blasts my eardrum.

Meadow hops down from her scratching post and comes to sit on my lap, maybe sensing my distress. I pet her. The feel of her fur and the sound of her purring soothe my panic.

Maybe the transaction hasn't gone through yet. Maybe it's just a matter of canceling it instead of issuing a refund.

What kind of monster asks for a refund from a charity, anyway?

Meadow nudges her head into my palm, and I realize I'm frozen. I continue petting, and her purring resumes.

Today is her one-year adoption anniversary, and I thought I would celebrate by making a donation to the charity who matched her with me. It guts me to have to ask them to cancel a huge donation but what am I supposed to do? They'll understand that it was an honest mistake, right?

I'd love to be the type of person who donates ten thousand dollars to a cat charity. But right now, I'm twenty-three, just out of college, and making the bare minimum at a marketing firm.

One day, I'll be the president of my own marketing firm, and it'll be so successful that I'll send massive donations to every cat rescue in the world without a second thought.

The hold music continues, and I pet my beautiful calico soulmate for a long time until she has enough and walks away.

My stomach grumbles. I get up to make breakfast, imagining the transaction soaring through cyberspace, getting closer and closer to my credit card.

I boil water, make instant coffee and instant oatmeal, and stir them slowly. What's taking so long?

I pull out a bar stool and get started on the oatmeal.

The hold music stops. There's a click.

"Hello, Feline Pawadise, this is Veronica," the receptionist says in her deadpan tone.

"No!" I cry through a mouthful of oatmeal, my heart sinking. I swallow hard. "I mean, hi, I was on hold to talk to Devi?"

"Oh. She must be busy. Hang on."

Back to the obnoxious hold music.

Devi's name swims at the back of my mind, making my heart beat a little faster. I met her the day I adopted Meadow, and I've thought about her a lot since then—wondering about all the things I did and didn't do. Wondering if I read her correctly. Wondering if we would cross paths again. Hoping, really.

The music stops. There's a click.

"Hello, Feline Pawadise, this is Veronica," the receptionist says.

I hang up, and scream into my apartment.

"I'm going there in person," I tell Meadow, who looks at me with a lot of judgment for that outburst. "I'm sorry. I'll buy a can of tuna for you on my way home, and we'll celebrate your big day."

I brush my teeth, then change out of my pajamas and into the same preppy outfit I wore to work yesterday—a short, black-and-yellow plaid skirt, long-sleeved black shirt, and black flats. It's formal for a cat rescue, but I'm too frazzled to try and piece together anything else. I pull my dark hair into a high ponytail, grab my bag and sunglasses, and head out the door.

It takes me half an hour to get there by bus. That's thirty whole minutes for the donation to go through on my credit card.

The transaction is definitely done by now. Shit. I guess I'm asking a charity for a ten-thousand dollar refund today.

Feline Pawadise is a nondescript unit at the back of a strip mall, nestled between a bagel shop and a pharmacy. Faded, peeling cat stickers cover the windows and glass door. They could use a face lift, but I guess it's nice to know that they use their donation money for the cats and not aesthetics.

I open the door, and step into a place that smells very strongly like cats and cleaning products. The reception desk is to the left. To the right, a few people work at desks that look like they came straight out of the 90s. On the opposite wall, a door leads to the back, which I passed through last time to see the cats and adopt Meadow.

I stride up to the reception desk. Veronica is a pale, middle-aged blond woman wearing a t-shirt with a faded picture of three kittens on it.

"Hi, Veronica, it's Sarah Chow," I say, a little calmer now that I've had thirty minutes to simmer down on the bus.

"Oh. Hi." Veronica doesn't seem surprised to see me here. Does anything faze her?

"Hi. I was just panicking to you on the phone. Can I please talk to Devi?"

"Sure, let me call her." She picks up the phone and punches in what I assume is an extension.

She waits. And waits.

Oh, for God's sake.

"Maybe you should go get her in person," I say. "Does she usually ignore her phone this much? What if she's on the floor of her office and needs help?"

Veronica ignores me. She hangs up, then dials again. And we wait.

The door to the back swings open, and a woman my age emerges carrying a blue binder. She's in tan, high-waisted cargo pants and a white tank top, a sliver of brown skin peeking through at her stomach. As she lays the binder on Veronica's desk, my gaze draws to her very toned arms. She's sporting a short, masculine cut that frames the angles of her face.

My heart stops. *Devi.*

She looks different from before—more confident, happier, and hot damn, that haircut will be the death of me.

I try to say hello but my mouth is dry.

"Devi, this is Sarah Chow," Veronica says flatly, returning her attention to her computer.

"Oh!" Devi exclaims, locking me with her dark gaze. She looks startled, and actually takes a step back. I furrow my brow, and she seems to catch herself. She stuffs her hands into her pockets, her face relaxing into a smile. "Right—Sarah—you just made that incredible donation."

My stomach seems to drop into my feet. "Um—"

"I couldn't believe it when I saw it," Devi continues. "I actually screamed. Didn't I, Dan?"

At a desk in the corner, Dan looks up, and humors her with a smile.

I try not to glare at him. This guy's crappy website design is the reason I'm here. Here, and about to shatter Devi's happiness.

This is the worst. I can't think of anything else I'd rather do less right now.

Devi looks at me, and something glimmers in her dark eyes. Her brow pinches. Does she remember me?

There's a pause while we look at each other. I forgot how beautiful she was. I made an idiot of myself the day

I adopted Meadow, stumbling over my words and blushing all over the place.

The phone rings at reception, and we break eye contact.

"So, how can I help you, Sarah?" Devi asks, sounding breathless. She plays with a feather-shaped pendant on her chest, drawing my gaze to her fingers.

Last time I was here, my shameless flirting had been cut short when I'd suddenly noticed the ring on her finger. It'd been mortifying. But today, her fingers are bare.

I blink, forcing myself to focus.

Am I doomed to keep embarrassing myself in front of her?

"Actually, I came here because I…" My throat seals. I don't want to say it. Do I have to say it?

Devi looks at me intensely, and it's easy to remember why I found her so irresistible. Her dark eyes hook me, making me forget my words.

"Do you want to come to my office?" she asks.

I step forward automatically. "Yeah, sure."

She leads me through the door and into the back. Distant meowing fills the hallway—tempting me as before to adopt every single cat here—and then it's muffled again when we push through a glass door into her office.

Her office is much nicer than the rest of the building. There's a window that peeks out onto a sidewalk, open slightly, a breeze rustling the six plants crowding the windowsill. She's strung fairy lights around the ceiling, and there are several paintings of beaches on the walls.

"Did you paint those yourself?" I ask, dropping my bag on a chair in the corner.

She lowers her gaze, looking shy. "How'd you know? Is it because they're terrible?"

"No, they're really good! I remember you telling me you were taking classes."

She smiles. "So you remember me."

"And you remember me."

She bites her lip, searching my face. "Why did you come here?"

"I—um—" Crap, I don't want to do this. "How have you been?"

"I've been good. Better than ever, actually." Devi steps closer, a teasing smile on her lips. "Is that why you came? To ask how I am?"

I shake my head. The light, floral scent of her perfume meets my nose, making me want a taste.

"I think I know why you're here," Devi says softly.

My insides hollow out. "You do?"

She nods. "I've thought about you too, Sarah. I've thought about how sorry I was to have to say no that day."

Oh my God. She thinks I came here to ask her out. I'm totally leading her on by acting all awkward.

But—wait—she's thought about me since then?

My heart skips a beat. Suddenly, the real reason I came here feels less important. "I was sorry it ended up that way too," I admit.

The smallest smile curves her lips. I can't get enough of how gorgeous she is—the way she tilts her head, the line of her collar bone, her muscular arms, the curve of her waist, down to her confident stance.

Sometimes, you find someone who you just can't get out of your head, no matter how you met, and no matter how much time you spend apart. Devi is that person for me. We met one time a whole year ago—and somehow, not a single date I've been on has ever matched up to the way I felt that day. The way we clicked. The way I couldn't stop smiling while we talked.

"When we met, I didn't know what I wanted," Devi says. "I thought I was happily engaged."

"Are you not engaged anymore, then?" I ask quietly.

She shakes her head. "We broke it off nearly a year ago."

My pulse quickens. Outside the open window, people walk by, talking and laughing. Everything outside of this office feels far away.

"I'm sorry," I say.

"It's okay. I'm better now."

"Good."

She swallows hard. "I wondered if I should contact you, but that would be inappropriate given that you're a… customer or whatever. But I couldn't get you out of my head. Something about the way you smiled at me, the way you made me feel wanted…"

I knew it. I could tell something was wrong in her relationship that day. I'd flirted with her without realizing she was engaged, and the bright way she responded made me think she was single. Then I saw her ring, and when I asked her who her lucky partner was, she'd shut down. She seemed sad, cut off, and had finished processing Meadow's adoption papers quickly.

"He was a guy," Devi says stiffly, like it's a struggle to get the words out. "I was engaged to a man. And I was totally kidding myself."

"Oh." I search for the right words. Is it too forward to ask about her sexuality? "Um, have you been able to do some self-reflection since breaking off the engagement?"

My heartbeat quickens as the office begins to feel smaller.

Devi nods. "I've been on dates with women since then. But I keep coming back to thinking about you. I wondered if I was building you up in my head, making you out to be… Like, you were my awakening, and so I wondered if you were more of an idea than a person."

"I was your awakening?" I ask, flattered.

"An important part of it, yes," she says without any shyness. She holds my gaze with blazing intensity, making me bite my lip.

"And now that we've met again… am I still just an idea?" I ask, my stomach fluttering in anticipation of the answer.

Her lips part. She shakes her head. With the way she's looking me up and down with a hungry gleam in her eyes, I'm suddenly glad I wore a skirt instead of sweatpants.

My lips tingle. After all this time of pining over her, I want nothing more than to take her in my arms and unravel her right now. Why do we have to be in an office with a glass door?

She feels closer than she did a moment ago. Have we both stepped in?

I glance over my shoulder, where the hall beyond the glass door is empty. I step closer to her until we're nose-to-nose.

Her breath catches. Her lips are parted, inviting me in.

I lean in, teasing her with the lightest brush of my lips. Her hand slides around my waist, holding me there.

The gentle brush of our lips sends a spark through me, making my head spin. Her breath hitches. Her fingers tighten on my waist.

"The things I want to do to you…" I whisper.

Footsteps click beyond her office door, and we both jump back.

What am I doing? I'm losing my mind. This is her workplace. This isn't the moment to make out, no matter how much we both want it.

"C-come in," Devi says, flushed. She turns away from me and crosses her arms, drawing a breath.

I can't help but smile. As frustrated as I am that we couldn't finish that kiss, I love that I made her look this undone without even doing much.

The door opens, and a familiar deadpan voice says, "Devi, I think your phone must be disconnected. I haven't been able to send anyone through to you all morning."

Yeah, no shit, I want to say. *It's why I'm here in person.*

Devi looks at the phone on her desk with a pinched brow. "Oh. I'll get Dan to look at it."

"There's a couple here wanting to adopt," Veronica says. "They'll probably need you soon. Sarah, did you get the donation sorted?"

"Get what sorted?" Devi asks.

My heart jumps into my throat. "Nothing," I say. "Actually, I was thinking—I—wanted to do more for Feline Pawadise. Do you need volunteers? Can I submit an application?"

Great, first I'm donating money I don't have, and now I'm volunteering time I don't have. Keep digging, Sarah.

"No, the refund," Veronica says.

I clench my fists, resisting the urge to shove her out the door and slam it.

"Refund?" Devi asks, her brow pinched.

I rub my hands over my face and take a deep breath. I guess I couldn't keep this a secret forever. What was I going to do, pay off the ten-thousand dollar donation on my credit card until the end of time?

No, as much as I want to shout at Veronica, it's not her fault. I'm being an idiot, and I have to get this sorted. Even if it risks whatever might have happened between Devi and me.

"I actually came here," I say to Devi, my voice a little shaky, "because I made that donation by mistake."

There's a terrible silence. I can feel my pulse in my neck. Somewhere, a cat meows.

"I'm sorry," I say, forcing the words past my numb lips. "I came here to ask for my donation amount to be changed to a hundred dollars, which is what I really meant to put, but you were so happy, and…"

Veronica sidles out of the office with a grimace, apparently realizing what she's done.

I want to die. Just crawl into the nearest hole and completely vanish.

Devi is painfully quiet. I feel the silence in my chest, suffocating. We're a stride apart, my back to the door, the sunlight beyond her window illuminating her from behind.

"You were so cute when you were excited, and I couldn't bring myself to crush that," I say, though that probably doesn't help.

"Is that why you came here?" Devi asks quietly.

I nod, squinting at the plants on her windowsill. "I tried to call but I couldn't get through, so…"

She covers her mouth with both hands. "I'm so embarrassed."

"You? Why are you embarrassed? I'm the one who made the mistake."

"I feel like an idiot!" Devi says. "I don't know why I assumed… Like, we've never had a donation that big, Sarah. Ever. Why would I assume it was on purpose?"

"Why *wouldn't* you?" I ask. "It's not your fault. I was groggy this morning and hadn't had coffee yet, and I just…" I type in the air with my fingers, miming my blunder.

"And were you serious about wanting to submit a volunteer application?" Devi asks.

My face is on fire. I think it's time to start looking for the nearest hole to crawl into.

"It wasn't why I came here," I admit, my voice barely coming out. I clear my throat.

She rubs her face. "Here I was thinking you wanted to…" She motions between the two of us with a finger. "This is mortifying."

"No," I say quickly. My heart is beating fast. There's a possibility that whatever sparked between the two of us is completely smothered, and the best thing would be for me to go back home to my cat and forget that kiss ever happened—but I loved that she confessed her feelings to me. I love that she's been thinking about me all this time, because I haven't stopped thinking about her either.

I can't ruin whatever was going on between us. I have to take a shot.

"Devi, would volunteering here give me a chance to spend more time with you?" I ask, my heart tripping over itself. "Because if that's the case, then yes, I'd like to volunteer here."

She stares at me for a long moment.

The pause is agonizing. I can't feel my legs.

Finally, her lips pull into a little smile. My heart lifts.

"The applications are at reception," she says.

"Cool." I hesitate. The way she's leaning against her desk is inviting, like I could step between her legs and stoop to kiss her.

Ugh, I want to finish that kiss but this office is all windows.

"And I can process that refund for you," Devi says.

My knees weaken for an entirely different reason. "Thank you. God, that amount would have killed me."

She smiles.

We stare at each other. Devi bites her lip, her gaze roaming down my body.

"Um, I guess I'll... get a volunteer application..." I jab a thumb over my shoulder.

Devi looks past me, and then around the office, as if searching for something. "Have I ever given you a tour of the facility?"

"A tour?" I furrow my brow in confusion. What's with the change of topic?

She steps closer. "Come on. I'll show you around."

"I was actually shown around last time I was here, when I adopted Meadow—"

Devi grabs my hand and sighs, pulling me along. I grab my bag from the chair in the corner on the way out of her office. We walk down the hall, our hands clasped, and I will my feet to cooperate so I don't trip.

"The adoptable cats are all down that way," she says loudly. "That's the room where we do health exams... And here's the storage closet."

Her fingers tighten around mine. My head spins as I grasp what's going on.

Devi opens the door. It's dark inside. Bins and towels are stacked on shelves along the left and right walls.

She pulls me inside, and when she turns around and faces me, there's a pause. My pulse is racing. My brain is frantically churning, trying to work out how bold she wants me to be, and I'm aching, wanting...

I kick the door shut, plunging us into darkness. The only light comes from a tiny crack between the bottom of the door and the tile floor.

"If you want to spend time with me, you could also just ask me out," she whispers. "You don't have to submit a volunteer application."

My insides erupt into dance. "Okay," I say, breathless. "Do you want to go out with me?"

She puts her soft, warm hands on either side of my face, and closes the distance between us. Though it's dark, I can sense her face hovering before mine.

"Yes," she whispers into my lips. "I've been dreaming of you asking me out for a year."

Her breath is sweet, her perfume intoxicating. After all of the dates I've been on, it's amazing how she's lingered in my mind—this perfect woman whose smile brightened my day, whose laugh stayed in my head like a song I couldn't forget, whose sorrows I wanted to fix with a hug and a kiss.

Finally, I get her to myself—even if it's not in quite the way I expected.

I drop my bag on the floor and kiss her, parting her lips with my tongue. She lets out a gasp, and then I'm stumbling backward, and my back is pressed against the shelves, and her body is firmly against mine.

Oh, she's strong—and *bold*. Was this confidence here last time we met, simmering beneath the surface?

In the blackness, with the danger of being caught playing at my nerves, my senses are sharpened. My skin sizzles beneath her touch as she slips her hands under my shirt. I hold her to me, running my fingers up the curve of her waist, while our lips and tongues explore each other. She tastes minty and cool, and when she takes her lips away, I'm left wanting.

She bends to kiss my neck, making me hiss.

The darkness frees me to act on instinct, and I can feel my inhibitions dissipating. My lips and hands move on their own, feeling every inch of her. Her skin is soft beneath my palms, her muscles firm. The shelves press against my spine but I don't care. I could stand here making out with her for hours.

Devi reaches one hand around to my ass while the other palms my breast. She rubs her thumb back and forth, teasing my nipple through my shirt and bra.

She's driving me wild. I can't take it. I grab her tank top and the sports bra under it, lifting it high enough to expose her breasts. She gasps.

Nobody had better need this closet in the next few minutes.

I bend to take her nipple in my mouth, swirling my tongue.

Devi stifles a cry, arching into me. "Sarah, that's so good…"

I hold her waist, keeping her in place as I lick and suck. The way she's squirming turns me on, making me wet.

Footsteps thump on the other side of the door, and we both freeze. I straighten up.

The steps continue, fading down the hallway, and Devi lets out a breath.

"Sarah, I need you," she whispers, pulling my chin back to her. With the other hand, she's teasing my thigh beneath the hem of my skirt. "Can I touch you?"

God, I love how bold she's being. It's such a turn-on.

My brain is telling me this is a bad idea, and we should stop. We're in public. The door doesn't lock. But my body is screaming yes. I want her fingers on me. I want to make her moan.

"Yes," I whisper, pulling her in for another deep kiss.

She lifts my skirt and reaches into my underwear, and as her fingers slip between my legs, I can't stop the gasp from escaping.

My insides are burning with desire. Devi is a different person from the last time we met—bold, confident, getting what she wants. I want her in my bed on top of me instead of in a storage closet.

For now, this will have to do.

I fumble for her pants, unbuttoning them so I can get my hand inside. As I touch her, she stifles a cry against my neck. Her fingers move faster.

I'm dizzy, using the shelves for balance. In the darkness, her little moans and hitches of breath are amplified.

"I want to taste you," she whispers, taking her hand away and bending down.

I whimper incoherently as she kneels on the floor and pushes my skirt up. She tugs my underwear down, and teases me with her cool tongue. My brain dissolves into a haze, and I sink down against the shelves, gripping it for support. I'm lost in the feel of her tongue on me. The whole world becomes just her.

Her tongue moves faster, and I roll my hips, letting my body respond to her automatically.

Heat builds inside me. My legs start to tremble, and I grab her face, pulling her back up to my lips. "Come here."

"But I want to—" she starts to protest, and I silence her with a kiss.

I slip my hand into her underwear, and she moans into my mouth. Her fingers find their way under my skirt, and she moves her fingers quickly, making me gasp.

We move faster until my brain seems to dissipate. Heat builds inside me, growing more intense, and I gasp into Devi's mouth.

"You close?" she whispers, her other hand wound tightly in my hair.

"Yeah," I say, breathless.

"Me too—" Her words are smothered when I kiss her hard, my body giving in.

I lean into her, my knees weakening as my climax courses through me. I gasp into her mouth, trying to stay quiet. The orgasm sets off Devi, who doesn't do as good a job staying quiet. She cries out, her voice filling the small space.

We lean against each other, sweaty, panting, and my whole body is tingling with pleasure.

Footsteps thump past the door, and we both freeze until they're gone.

I let out a laugh, unable to help it. "That was so hot," I whisper. "I've never done it anywhere but in a bedroom before."

"Same," Devi says, laughing too.

I fumble for my bag, and it takes me a moment to find it on the floor. I pass her my phone. "What's your number?"

The light from my phone illuminates her face, and she's giving me the most radiant smile.

A minute later, Devi sneaks me to the staff bathroom so I can use it to clean up and tame my sex hair. When I'm done, we walk back to the reception area, where everybody looks at us. Veronica, Dan, and the other people at their desks openly stare, maybe wondering why I've been here for so long—and why we disappeared from Devi's office.

Heat rises in my face.

"I—I'll adjust your donation amount to a hundred dollars," Devi tells me, avoiding everyone's gaze.

"Thanks. And, um—I'll take one of these." I grab a volunteer application from a stack at the reception desk, intending to think about it before I dive in with a commitment I'm not ready for.

"Bye, then," Devi says, breathless.

Her short hair is a mess. She's clammy and flush-faced. Her shirt is still twisted. It's totally obvious what we were doing.

I grin. "Call me."

I wink, and Devi bites her lip.

"Thanks for your help, Veronica," I say, saluting her. If it weren't for her, and all of the other mishaps that led me to come to this office, I wouldn't have met Devi again. I wave to the other person I have to thank, smiling. "And Dan? Great job on the website design."

Thank you for supporting an indie author by reading this collection of short stories! If you enjoyed them, I'd like to invite you to check out my other books. Turn the page for a special sneak peek of one of them!

Mermaids of Eriana Kwai Series
Ice Massacre
Ice Crypt
Ice Kingdom

From Fan to Forever

The Valkyrie's Daughter

Cougar Woods (Eternally Hers collection)

I love to connect with my readers! Find me at:
tianawarner.com
instagram.com/tianawarner
twitter.com/tianawarner
tiktok.com/@tiana_warner

Enjoy this special sneak peek of…

FROM FAN
TO
FOREVER

From Fan to Forever, an age-gap celebrity romance, is
available now from Ylva Publishing.

Chapter One
Dragging Home a Moose Floatie

I've been away for one night, and in that time, my street has turned into a movie set.

Easing my car to a stop behind an orange-and-white-striped barricade, I gape at the crowds, white tents, and trailers filling the intersection in front of my apartment. A metal fence surrounds the area like a crime scene.

My gut twists and I tighten my grip on the steering wheel. On any other day, this would be exciting, but all I want right now are my bathtub, bed, and painkillers. Today is supposed to be a blissful day off before I have to start my master's thesis research, not a daring crusade to get to my front door.

A crane lifts a camera high into the air, where ropes and wires crisscross above the set. Is that a zip-line leading into my favorite pizza place? What kind of over-the-top action flick is this?

My third-floor balcony is visible from here, with its two wooden patio chairs and the wilted hydrangeas that Abby and I never remember to water. In the window beside it, my dark bedroom curtains are shut, as always.

Staying home to spy on the set would have been more fun than that stupid-ass camping trip, but here I am, sweaty and hungover.

Scowling, I back up my rusty, old SUV and circle the block, searching for a way into the parkade.

In the rearview, my reflection is waxy and pale, and my short, sandy hair is so greasy that it's a shade darker, like I've just come out of the shower. Self-loathing has sucked the confidence from my posture.

Yeah, I was an idiot, but in my defense, Julia was flirting with me and totally into it.

"'Ooh, Rachel, let's get naked in the lake together,'" I say to the windshield, mimicking her sultry tone.

It's hard to believe that the unspoken thing between us is over—late-night study sessions, hanging out after class, inside jokes, our shared suffering as we both go after master's degrees in medical physics. She'd quickly become a good friend, and after she found out I'm a lesbian, she started asking questions about my love life and wanting to hang out more—like she was curious. Like maybe she thought she wasn't straight and wanted to explore some things.

Months of anticipation, over in one night, leaving me hollow.

This camping trip was supposed to be a big end-of-term celebration for our department. For Julia and me, it was a culmination, an excuse to get drunk and spend a couple of nights together.

The tension between us was ready to snap, and it did—so hard that it gave me whiplash.

I rub my temple, weaving through the streets and trying to get to my parkade. The movie set takes up way more space than it has any right to, forcing me to make a wide perimeter. As soon as I figure out how to get to my apartment, I'm filling the bathtub and dropping in a glittery bath bomb. Since I left yesterday morning, I've swum in a lake, gotten sweaty, been briefly rained on, and walked through a lot of spiderwebs, so I need a good scrub. My skin is so sticky that my shirt is plastered to my back.

After circling for ten minutes, I resign myself to parking three blocks away. I drag my camping gear down the road—the bag of damp clothes, the cooler of food I never ate, and a mostly deflated moose floatie. The early summer heat wave adds more sweat to what's already dried to my skin. I'd better not run into any neighbors in the elevator, or they'll be in for a treat when they get a whiff of me.

I swipe my fob to get inside, and before I open the door, laughter erupts behind me.

I whirl around, ready to tell off whoever is laughing at me for dragging camping gear down the street, but the sound is coming from the movie set.

A metal fence separates me from the set—they have to keep us peasants out, obviously—and white tents block most of my view beyond it. Between two tents is a gap that tunnels my vision to a point.

My heart does a wild, out-of-control flip, knocking me off balance so that I have to grab the door handle to stay standing.

Cate Whitney is on the other side of the fence, talking to a tattooed guy with a boom mic.

Cate. Whitney.

I forget how to breathe.

In her early forties and well-established on the A-list, she carries herself with easy confidence. She's rocking a badass black and brown steampunk outfit, including a corset, thigh-high fishnet stockings, a frilly skirt that exposes her thighs in front and hangs calf-length in the back, and a top hat with goggles resting on the brim. Her shoulder-length blond hair is in soft curls, and her white skin has a warm glow, like she's been in the tropics. She's wearing her signature mischievous smirk, her makeup drawing attention to her sharp cheekbones and ice-blue eyes.

How is it possible for anyone to be so attractive? I guess that's why she ended up in Hollywood. She's the type of woman who can rock a tux better than any man and a Valentino dress better than a runway model.

Seeing her in person sparks memories of pivotal moments in my life, making my chest flutter.

When I saw her kiss a woman in a 2000s historical drama, that was the moment I knew. Though the movie was fiction and the actors were straight, their love felt so real, sending butterflies through me. I wanted what those women had—their passion for each other, the connection that reached beyond friendship, the purity of their love.

I asked out my crush after seeing it, and she said yes.

On our fourth date, we watched that same movie together, and I made out with a girl for the first time.

So I'm not being dramatic when I say that Cate Whitney changed my life.

Now, standing with the poise of a goddess, that woman is ten feet away. She's deep in conversation with the guy with the boom mic, but that doesn't stop her from looking past him and meeting my eye.

Why? Why does she have to see me when I look like I climbed out of a dumpster?

Reflexively, I offer an awkward half-smile, which she returns.

My insides flip. This is either the greatest thing ever to happen to me or the worst, depending on whether she can smell me from this distance.

Regaining feeling in my legs, I whip open the door of my building and hurtle myself inside, then grab my camping gear and drag it in after me. The moose floatie smacks the door frame on the way in.

Cate freaking Whitney is feet away from me, filming a movie.

I hyperventilate my way up to my apartment and unlock the door with trembling hands. The familiar smell of home hits my nose—sweet-orange essential oil diffusing on the kitchen island, woven with layers of shampoo, burnt toast, and cheap coffee. Abby must be up.

I dump my camping gear and rush through the kitchen and living room toward the balcony. The apartment is as I left it, cluttered and full of low-maintenance plants. My laptop, heap of textbooks, and blanket nest are untouched on my side of the couch. Trinkets from travels, books, and pictures of friends and family take up every surface. It's disorganized—Abby prefers the term *eclectic*—but it's home.

I slide open the patio door and burst through to spy on the movie set.

The view is awe-inspiring. They've built a clockwork storefront over my favorite coffee shop. White tents and trailers, the back of wooden structures, and a lot of expensive film equipment clutter the intersection.

From the depths of the apartment, footsteps pad closer, and Abby says, "You smell like worn-off deodorant and sunscreen. I thought you weren't coming home until tomorrow."

"Cate Whitney is down there," I whisper-shout, scanning the dozens of people milling about the set.

"Fuck off!" Abby screams, rushing beside me to peer over the balcony.

I clap a hand over her mouth. "Shh!"

Abby pries my hand off. "You *saw* her?"

"Right as I was coming inside." I wrack my brain for the last headline I saw about Cate Whitney. "She must be filming *Clockwork Curie*."

There she is. She's with a group of people behind the cameras, pointing at a monitor and nodding. She's easy to spot because of the outfit but also because of that abnormally attractive Hollywood look. What is *with* that?

"Clockwork what?" Abby says.

"It's a steampunk movie about Marie Curie," I whisper. "The scientist. We were talking about it in class not long ago."

As if a high-budget movie about science hero Marie Curie isn't awesome enough, they had to go and cast Cate Whitney as the lead. Excuse me while I cry feminist tears.

"Abby, she was, like, ten feet away from me," I say, making sure she understands the situation.

I peel my gaze away from the set. Abby is wearing a smart navy blazer and no pants. Her thick, dark hair is styled to emphasize its natural waves, she's wearing makeup, and her oversized glasses are unusually free of smudges.

"What's up with you?" I ask.

"Virtual job interview."

"What company?"

"Enough about me. Are you going to try and meet Cate?"

My heart jumps at the question like I've just been dive-bombed by an angry crow. "What? No. She's working."

"Girl, you've been obsessed with her since before you knew you were a lesbian. Remember the magazine pictures taped to your high school locker?"

"Shh!" I say, dragging Abby inside. I slam the patio door and round on her. "I can't just walk up to her!"

"Sure you can. Rachel, this is the universe bringing you an opportunity," she says, picking lint off her blazer. "Seize it."

I rub my tired eyes. Cate Whitney really is a queer icon. Between her film roles, her wardrobe, and being an outspoken ally, I'm positive that if someone were to poll all of the lesbians and ask them to rank their top celebrity crushes, she would win the popular vote.

I guess I could try to say hi to my hero. The prospect sends a nervous thrill through my chest. "What would I even say?"

Abby opens the bamboo privacy screen we use as a backdrop during video calls, which conveniently masks the surrounding disaster. "I don't know. *Big fan of your work*?"

"Ugh, that's so normal."

"If you want her to remember you for something abnormal, fine, but I think you're better off sticking with something average here."

"Fair enough." I hesitate, heart thumping. Then I shake my head firmly. "No, I can't. It's too awkward."

"You have to!"

Carefully, she places her laptop in front of the dirty dishes and unfolded laundry on the kitchen table.

"You just want me out of the apartment during your interview," I say.

"Well, yes, but I also want you to seize the day. Do it. I'm not letting you back in until you say at least one word to her."

"Excuse me?" I say, laughing.

"You heard me, Rachel Henrietta Janssen," she says severely. "I'm shoving you out the door and bolting it until you succeed."

"What if I'm not allowed on se—"

"I double dare you," she says in a girly tone reminiscent of our high school slumber parties.

"Oh, shut it."

She makes chicken noises and I throw a tissue box at her. It bounces off her chest.

"Did Amelia Earhart let people stop her from achieving her goals?" she asks, waving her arms.

"Amelia Earhart died while achieving her goal, Abby."

"Beside the point. You'll thank me later."

I chew my lip. As uncomfortable as it would be to approach a celebrity, I would live my life in deep regret if I didn't do it. Cate Whitney is more than a celebrity crush. She's a legend, an icon who helped me discover my sexuality and come out.

"It's not like you're the only one. I saw a couple of girls leaning over the fence to get pics with the actors last night," Abby says, a wry smile on her lips, like she knows I'm at my tipping point.

I can't help it—my face breaks into a grin. "Dare accepted. I'll ask her to sign the back of my phone."

I grab a permanent marker from the jar on the counter.

"An autograph? What kind of person in this day and age—" Abby stops, probably remembering that the alternative is to ask for a selfie, and I hate having my picture taken. "I guess having Cate Whitney's signature on the back of your phone would be cool."

"Hell yeah, it would. Do I have time to shower before your interview?"

"Yes!" Abby squeals in excitement. She opens her laptop and settles into a chair, checking the position of the privacy screen. "You've got twenty-four minutes to get out of here. Why are you back early, anyway? How was camping?"

"Good luck with your interview," I shout, racing to the bathroom.

My attempt to dodge her question doesn't work, and she chases after me.

"How was camping, Rachel?"

"Fine!"

"Liar."

Ugh, she's too perceptive.

Before I can shut the door, she wedges her hand between it and the frame.

"What happened with Julia, Rachel?"

*

You have reached the end of
Chapter One of *From Fan to Forever*!

Find this book and others at tianawarner.com

Thank you for reading!